"*You* Advert... Answered That Ad In Good Faith. And Now I Need You To Fulfill Your Obligations."

Heart pounding, she pulled out her trump card. With what she desperately hoped were seductive movements, she eased onto his lap and looped her wrists around his neck.

"Just so there's no question in your mind," she whispered, "I want you to know that I intend to keep my part of the bargain. *Every* part of the bargain."

She brushed her lips against his slowly.

"I want to be your wife, Abel Greene."

Dear Reader,

Happy Valentine's Day! This season of love is so exciting for us here at Silhouette Desire that we decided to create a special cover treatment for each of this month's love stories—just to show how much this very romantic holiday means to us.

And what a fabulous group of books we have for you! Let's start with Joan Elliott Pickart's MAN OF THE MONTH, *Texas Moon*. It's romantic and wonderful—and has a terrific hero!

The romance continues with Cindy Gerard's sensuous *A Bride for Abel Greene*, the next in her NORTHERN LIGHTS BRIDES series, and also with Elizabeth Bevarly's *Roxy and the Rich Man*, which launches her new miniseries about siblings who were separated at birth, THE FAMILY McCORMICK.

Christine Pacheco is up next with *Lovers Only*, an emotional and compelling reunion story. And Metsy Hingle's dramatic writing style shines through in her latest, *Lovechild*.

It's always a special moment when a writer reaches her **25the book milestone**—and that's just what Rita Rainville has done in the humorous and delightful Western, *City Girls Need Not Apply*.

Silhouette Desire—where you will always find the very best love stories! Enjoy them all....

Lucia Macro

Senior Editor

Please address questions and book requests to:
Silhouette Reader Service
U.S.: 3010 Walden Ave., P.O. Box 1325, Buffalo, NY 14269
Canadian: P.O. Box 609, Fort Erie, Ont. L2A 5X3

CINDY GERARD
A BRIDE FOR ABEL GREENE

SILHOUETTE *Desire*®
Published by Silhouette Books
America's Publisher of Contemporary Romance

This book is dedicated to my agent, Maria Carvainis,
for her insight and support, and to my editor,
Lucia Macro, for her vision and
irrepressible enthusiasm.

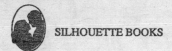 SILHOUETTE BOOKS

ISBN 0-373-76052-3

A BRIDE FOR ABEL GREENE

Copyright © 1997 by Cindy Gerard

Printed in U.S.A.

Books by Cindy Gerard

Silhouette Desire

The Cowboy Takes a Lady #957
Lucas: The Loner #975
*The Bride Wore Blue #1012
*A Bride for Abel Greene #1052

*Northern Lights Brides

CINDY GERARD

If asked "What's your idea of heaven?" Cindy Gerard would say a warm sun, a cool breeze, pan pizza and a good book. If she had to settle for one of the four she'd opt for the book, with the pizza running a close second. Inspired by the pleasure she's received from the books she's read and her longtime love affair with her husband, Tom, Cindy now creates her own warm, evocative stories about compelling characters and complex relationships.

All that reading must have paid off, because since winning the Waldenbooks Award for Bestselling Series Romance for a First-Time Author, Cindy has gone on to win the prestigious Colorado Romance Writers' Award of Excellence, *Romantic Times* W.I.S.H. awards, Career Achievement and Reviewer's Choice nominations, and the Romance Writers of America's RITA nomination for Best Short Contemporary Romance.

NORTHERN LIGHTS
Brides

Northern Minnesota is a land of sparkling glacial lakes and forests that stretch as far as the eye can see. Fortunately, civilization has not yet marred its remote and intrinsic beauty. In any given spot, on any given lake, images of free-spirited Indian warriors riding spotted ponies through the tree line come unbidden, as the past collides with the present.

Shadows of turn-of-the-century French fur traders and hardworking loggers weave like the wind through the pine. At night, in a secluded bay, when the moon dances on the water and the stars shimmer in an inky sky, the Aurora Borealis mystifies, intensifying the sense of wonder in this very special place.

Come with us to Legend Lake, where its people are as in tune with the North Country's uncompromising beauty as they are enmeshed in the past. And like many before them, become enamored by the mystery of the Northern Lights.

Experience the beauty, and live all three captivating romances in the NORTHERN LIGHTS BRIDES TRILOGY as they unfold.

One

She'd been reduced to talking to herself. Out loud. It would have scared her, but that would have been redundant. She was already scared, good and scared, and she didn't want her little brother to know it.

"Maybe you're being too dramatic. Maybe you really aren't lost. Yeah, and maybe the sun doesn't set in the west," Mackenzie Kincaid mumbled to herself through chattering teeth and wondered when enough was finally going to be enough. In her opinion the irony was excessive. Only the cruelest twist of fate would lead them out of one life-threatening situation smack into the middle of another.

"You've come too far to let a little cold and snow do you in now, Kincaid," she told herself, in a staunch attempt to downplay the subzero windchill and deepening snow. Still, her brother's crude take on the situation pretty well summed it up: it sucked…big-time.

"There's an up side here," she insisted, again to herself,

clinging by a hangnail to what was left of her optimism. "You're getting an education."

In the past half hour, for instance, she'd learned that she'd never really had a handle on the word *cold*. Between this Minnesota snowstorm and her brother's glacial glares, she had a darn good grip on it now. If the frigid wind and the snow, caked around her ankles and sticking to her jeans, didn't freeze her solid, Mark, with the rebellious insolence only a brooding fifteen-year-old could master, would probably do the deed. Beside her, he plodded through two-foot drifts of white powder with all the enthusiasm of a member of the Donner party.

"Is all this really necessary?" she asked skyward, wrestling with the weight of her desperate decision to bring them here, the weight of the lie she was about to tell— and the more tangible weight of the nylon duffel bag that held everything she owned. Mark, his dark straggly hair crusted with—surprise—more snow, struggled with his own duffel. His top priority, though, was clutched protectively against his chest: the boom box he'd lugged all the way from L.A. and now guarded like precious metal.

Tugging the hood of her lightweight red jacket back into place, Mackenzie braced against a bone-chilling wind that took sadistic pleasure in whipping icy shards of snow in her face.

"Buck up, Kincaid," she demanded, making herself talk to keep panic from overtaking her. "You're going to get through this. Yes, you're cold. Yes, you're exhausted. But you can't let it beat you. Too much is at stake."

Not the least of which was their lives.

It seemed like a lifetime since she'd dragged Mark onto that bus, both of them packing enough uncertainties to pave a transcontinental highway. The thirty-six-hour trip had been brutal as they'd left sunny Southern California behind, crossed miles of parched desert, untamed mountains and winter-barren Midwest plains to end up here: the edge of the Arctic, in the guise of northern Minnesota.

She'd counted on the location to be remote. Remote was the biggest part of its appeal. What she hadn't counted on was getting caught in the middle of the storm of the century, or that they'd get lost in the brunt of it.

"Some people would look at this as an adventure," she suggested to Mark through chattering teeth, and she wondered if her lips were as blue as her brother's.

As a mood lifter, her suggestion was a major stretch. Mark wasn't buying it. Not that he verbalized his opinion. Fortunately he'd stopped verbalizing about an hour ago— just before he'd managed to alienate himself from the only human being in the bus terminal who'd had a four-wheel-drive and a sympathetic smile. If he'd mouthed off one more time, the bushy but amiable logger they'd run into at the Canadian border in Bordertown might have withdrawn his offer to drive them the extra thirty miles to their final destination.

"His cabin's about half a mile down that lane," the Paul Bunyon look-alike had claimed, after Mackenzie had told him where they wanted to go.

Cabin. What was left of the romantic in her had brightened at the picture that word conjured, until he'd added, "I'd drive you down there myself, but the man's a mite particular who he invites on his property. You folks don't waste any time walking up that lane, now. This storm promises to be a beaut."

Promises to be? Mackenzie had thought, as the man dropped them at the narrow opening in the forest and ground the gears on his rural assault vehicle, sending snow flying in his wake. If what they were experiencing now was a *promise,* she wasn't sure she wanted to stick around to see the real thing. And his repeated, "Now you're *sure* it's him you want to see?" had rattled her to the point that her doubts about coming here were now as numerous as the snowflakes.

"Not that you can back out now," she said as she hiked the duffel higher on her shoulder. "Not now that you've gotten this far."

And how far was that, exactly? She squinted through the wind-whipped snow. It had been a good half hour since the truck's taillights had disappeared. They still hadn't reached anything that resembled a clearing—let alone hinted at a sign of warmth or welcome.

"Of course, considering that you can barely see your hand in front of your face," she muttered, and made a swipe at the swirling, stinging snow that brought tears to her eyes, "you could have trudged past the Empire State Building and not spotted it."

Her feeble attempts at blowing off the seriousness of their situation were wearing thin. So was her hope. Ever since she'd lost the feeling in her toes, she'd been fighting panic, and she was afraid it might get the best of her until, moments later, she made out the outline of a roof nestled among the snow-shrouded pine and winter-barren birch.

She took a stumbling step closer.

"Thank you," she whispered, near tears, when the frame of a cabin took shape.

It wasn't just your basic hermit's cabin that she'd have gladly settled for at this point, either. It was a masterpiece of architectural design and beckoning warmth. Currier and Ives couldn't have painted a prettier picture. A high, peaked roof, laden with snow, topped the impressive log structure. Pale, muted light shimmered from behind a multitude of tall, frosty windows; smoke spiraled from a massive stone and mortar chimney, promising a toasty warm welcome.

Spirited high-fives would have been in order—if she hadn't spotted the wolf a split second later.

"Omigod," she whispered and stopped breathing.

The animal was huge. Every instinct she owned told her it was also hungry. Silver-gray eyes gleaming with predatory intent focused directly on her. Its charcoal and gray coat was matted with snow, yet the white of bared fangs was unmistakable—as was its low, warning growl. It stood at least four feet high at the shoulders, weighed over a hundred pounds. And for the life of her, Mackenzie couldn't shake the hysterical notion that she must look like a nineties version of what had once been her favorite fairy tale.

You had *to wear red...and it* had *to have a hood,* she thought fatalistically, as she shoved Mark behind her.

"Don't move," she whispered around the lump that was her heart jammed in her throat. "Don't...don't do anything. Just...just stay calm."

Mark's reed-thin body was as stiff as an icicle behind her. "What's it doing?"

"I...don't know. Watching, I guess. Maybe it's as afraid of us as we are of it."

Her brother's snort relayed how much stock he took in that notion. Her common sense agreed, and when the wolf inched a slinking step toward them, she ditched her *don't move* tactics like a bad habit.

"Run!" she shouted and gave Mark a hard shove toward the cabin, some twenty yards away. Then she threw her duffel. The animal agilely sidestepped the flying nylon and stalked a step closer.

She hadn't had time to register that Mark hadn't budged, when, in an unexpected show of concern, he stepped protectively in front of her.

"Mark, no!"

He wasn't listening. He was busy launching his own duffel.

Her hopes rose, then stalled out, when it, too, landed

short of the target. The predator crouched lower, its belly dragging in the snow, and began to circle.

She choked back a sob. She'd dragged Mark out of L.A., kicking and screaming, to keep him from getting killed—and now they both might die here instead. *Die.* The word rang with the finality of a funeral dirge, until Mark raised his treasured boom box over his head, hauled back and let it fly.

The radio hit a glancing blow to the wolf's back foot. Yipping in surprise, the animal crow-hopped into the cover of the forest.

It was the only incentive she needed. "Run!" she shouted, grabbed Mark's hand and stumbled at a labored sprint toward the cabin.

They hadn't gotten more than a few yards when she put on the breaks. A scream ripped from her throat as she jerked Mark to a stop beside her—then covered her mouth with her hand to stop another scream.

A moving mountain stalked menacingly toward them.

She couldn't move. Couldn't think past her shock, couldn't see past her fear, as adrenaline and stark terror teamed up to form one hysteria-induced conclusion: Sasquatch lives!

She felt like she was living through a badly edited montage of every horror movie she'd ever seen. Each corner they turned threw another threat in their path—this last one might be the most dangerous of them all.

Eyes as feral and black as a nightmare gleamed with unrelenting territorial anger beneath a knot of dark wool pulled low over his brow. A double-bladed ax was balanced over a shoulder that was as broad as a linebacker's and as matted with snow as the rest of his bulky body. And just in case she had any doubt that he represented a threat to life and limb, a knife, the blade of which was long, mean and surgically sharp, extended below a broad leather belt that sheathed it.

Compared to this ax-toting, frost-breathing, knife-wielding giant, the wolf seemed as threatening as a puppy.

Long, terrifying moments passed before Mackenzie finally convinced herself she was confronting a man, not a monster. Not that it made much difference at this point. He looked mad and he looked mean. And as she stood there, thinking that she'd never weighed the merits of dying of fright versus getting hacked to death, Mark sprang into action. With a banshee yell that ricocheted through the forest, he launched himself at the giant's midsection.

She screamed Mark's name.

The man only grunted in surprise when Mark head-butted him, and with an effortless swipe of his arm he dumped him head-first into a snow drift.

Mark came up spitting mad. He was wry and he was street smart, but he wouldn't make a good match for a wind sock. He was also determined to get himself killed. He lunged again, this time wrapping his thin arms around the big man's booted feet.

The maneuver caught the man off guard. The ax went flying. With the momentum of a tree falling, he landed in the snow with a thud, Mark hanging on as tightly as a flea on a dog's back.

Mackenzie didn't stop to wonder if the self-defense classes she'd recently taken were worth the money. She just knew that her little brother was in trouble. She pounced on the man's back, hooked an arm over his eyes and locked her legs around his waist.

"Let him go!" she shouted between frosty, labored breaths, and went to work on his throat.

He growled something short and crude then reached over his head, grabbed her by her jacket and hauled her off his back like she wasn't any more substantial than a lint ball.

She landed beside Mark with an "uff" that knocked the wind out of her and sent a star or two twinkling around the perimeters of her vision. When she could breath again and focus, her gaze connected with eyes as black as onyx, as hard as flint.

On his back next to her, still kicking and swinging like a featherweight, Mark spit snow and hurled names at the man who knelt above them.

"Just hold still damn it," he snarled, pinning them down with ease.

Mackenzie swiped snow from her face with the back of her wrist and glared as if she wasn't about to wet her pants with fear. "Let us go."

He didn't budge. Not that she'd expected him to. And until he decided to ease up, their only hope for escape was her wits—which Mark would be quick to point out meant they were in deep weeds.

"This is not a wise thing for you to do," she blurted out with as much authority as she could muster. "Just…just let us go—right now—or you're going to be in big trouble, mister."

A dark brow lowered beneath the black wool of his stocking cap. "*I'm* going to be in trouble? You may not have noticed. *I'm* the one on top."

"Look," she said, determined to ignore the obvious and get them out of this fix. "My husband…" She groped for words and came up with the trucker's. "He's real particular about who he invites on our property. Trust me, you don't want him to find you here. And if anything happens to us, he'll come looking for you," she added for good measure and prayed that the lie would trigger a reaction.

It did. More than she'd figured on. Between his stocking cap and the jacket buttoned tightly around his neck she couldn't see much of his face. But she could see his eyes—and the coldness there was devastating.

"You're telling me this is your property?"

His voice was dangerously soft, yet black-water deep.

She brazened it out, sticking to the lie like an ink stain to white silk. "Mine and my husband's."

"Yours and your...husband's. And who might this husband be?"

His skepticism was unmistakable. So was his impatience. Yet his hold loosened marginally. She took it as a positive sign. Shooting Mark a warning look to keep quiet, she compounded the lie. "Abel...Abel Greene."

He blinked once, slowly, his breath shooting frost from his nostrils like smoke from twin chimneys. "Abel Greene doesn't have a wife."

The calm deadly assurance of his statement sent her heart knocking.

"That...that may be true," she said, backpedaling, very aware of the strength and breadth of the broad, gloved hand flattened between her breasts. "But it's also about to change. We...he...Abel and I...we're getting married."

Something—surprise, disbelief and, if she read it right, resignation—flickered in his eyes before they raked her face with a long, slow and uncomfortably thorough assessment.

"You're not...hell. Don't tell me you're Mackenzie Kincaid."

Even as he asked, and her wary silence answered, he slowly shook his head.

He closed his eyes, uttered a short, concise oath. With a heavy breath he leaned back on his heels, letting her go so fast it took her a moment to register that she was free. Still another before it sank in that he knew who she was.

She scrambled to sit up, sifting through a dozen reasons why he would know her name. Only one made sense. She fought it with everything that was left in her—until common sense forced her to face the cold, hard facts.

Only one man in this open-air deep freeze could possibly know who she was—and his name wasn't Santa Claus.

She studied his winter-cold eyes, his dark, dangerous scowl, his look of total and uncompromising displeasure, and accepted that this was the man she'd traveled halfway across the country to marry. This was the man who had advertised for a bride.

As the ultimate irony of the situation sank in, she couldn't decide if she should laugh with relief or cry in outrage. She probably would have done both if she hadn't felt so much like screaming. In truth, though, she didn't have it left in her to do anything but stare.

She'd envisioned *old and hairless*. She'd imagined *burly and bushy*. She'd been prepared for anything but *mean*. The jury was still out on that one, but she tried to rationalize that since they'd just attacked him, his reaction was probably justified. Rationalizing, however, didn't help. She'd had too much. Too much fear, too much anxiety, too much everything.

An even break. That's all she'd wanted. That's all she'd needed to pull this off. She wasn't going to get it—not from the powers that be and not from him.

His eyes were as hard as diamonds. As dangerous as a cornered animal. Only the bottom line kept her from giving it up, begging him to forget the whole thing and hightailing it back to L.A. They couldn't go back. She needed Abel Greene.

He didn't know it yet, but he was going to be their savior. This place was going to be their sanctuary. It took only one swift, graphic memory to reinforce the necessity of coming here: the boy lying in his own blood on the street in front of their apartment.

The brutal picture was the push she needed to get focused again. But there was a problem. She'd maxed out on her self-control quotient. The last thirty-six hours had extracted too high a price. The last thirty minutes had redefined fear as she'd known it.

The next words out of her mouth confirmed she was slipping over the edge.

"I realize I'm not familiar with how things are done up here in Club Deep Freeze," she began, her voice escalating with her loss of restraint. "But if it's a local custom for prospective bridegrooms to maul the women they intend to marry, I'd like to lodge a protest!"

The last three words erupted on a yell that would have made an L.A. Lakers cheerleader proud. She was out of control and she knew it. All her fears, all her failures, erupted as reckless, righteous outrage.

Drawing a deep, ragged breath, she tried to settle herself down. She tried to gather her composure. She even tried to smile—but when his scowl only deepened, she did the one thing she couldn't have stopped if the earth had tilted and stopped turning.

With all the force of her one hundred five pounds—and emotions tried beyond all limits—she hauled back and slugged Abel Greene in his jutting masculine jaw.

She got a grunt of surprise for her efforts...and possibly a broken knuckle.

Past shock, beyond fear, she stared, as above the thick collar of his wool jacket, the veins on his neck expanded, full and pulsing. Beneath the edge of his black stocking cap, another vein bulged at his temple. And over the roar of blood rushing through her ears, she heard yet one more distinct, crude oath that in English or any other language could never be mistaken for "Glad you could make it."

Two

All things considered, Mackenzie took it as a positive sign that he didn't hit her back—and that he didn't leave them out in the cold. After digging around in the snow for their duffels, he walked them silently to the cabin. Once inside, he showed them where they could change into dry clothes, then settled them on a sofa by a warming fire. All of this was accomplished without a word or a direct glance her way.

That worked fine for her. She needed the time to settle herself down. To remind herself she was safe and warm—or would be as soon as the fire did its job. More importantly, she was here and so was Mark. She had to pull herself together if she was going to keep it that way.

Abel Greene was not a happy man. With good reason. He wasn't expecting her. He certainly wasn't expecting Mark.

Both she and Mark knew he'd written to call things off.

His letter had arrived the day before they were scheduled to leave L.A. He'd had second thoughts. He was sorry.

She hadn't had the luxury of second thoughts. And of the many things she was sorry for, the fact that she was going to start their relationship off with a lie topped the list. It went against the grain. But to save her brother, she wasn't beyond the deception. Abel Greene would never know she'd gotten his letter. As long as he thought she hadn't received it, she had justification for being here—and hopefully the ammunition to keep him from sending them back.

She shivered. They couldn't go back. They had nothing to go back to.

Wrapping her hands around the mug of hot coffee he'd given her, she snuggled inside her drab but dry, gray sweats and bundled up in the blanket he'd provided. Then she watched him in a silence caused as much by what she suspected was a mild case of shock, as by how he looked sans his Nanook the Barbarian battle gear.

He was not what she'd expected. Neither was he the throwback from the ice age that she'd thought he was at first glance. While still formidable in his silence and size, he was one of the most exotic looking men she'd ever seen.

As the fire crackled inside and the wind whistled around the windows outside, she took stock of him as he moved around the cabin. He was dressed in old, faded jeans and a chamois-colored flannel shirt that hugged his impressive body with the intimate familiarity of a possessive woman. And this man, upon close inspection, was a man any woman would love to possess—if she had the guts to try.

Mackenzie only prayed she had what it was going to take.

She'd always felt short-changed at five foot three, but she'd never felt dwarfed by anyone's presence. *Until now,* she amended, watching as he slipped into a pair of soft, doeskin moccasins. She would put him at three or four inches over six feet, his large-boned frame was two hundred pounds of masculine angles and lean, powerful muscle. Aside from all that length and strength, however, what repeatedly drew her attention, as he moved with catlike grace about the cabin, was his hair and the dramatic beauty of the face it framed.

Flowing like a straight, blue-black curtain midway down his back, it was tamed only by a navy bandanna he'd folded into a headband and tied around his high forehead. His thick, coarse hair showcased the bold, clean features of his face; his proud high cheekbones and blade-straight nose. Even if he hadn't had long hair, it was apparent that somewhere in his ancestry was a strong Native American gene or two. It didn't take much imagination to picture him wearing nothing but a loincloth, a war lance clutched in his hand, sitting astride a spotted pony as they splashed their way along the shoreline of a clear glacial lake.

The cabin, a story and a half of honey gold wood, lofty multiple-angled ceilings and open, unstructured rooms, reinforced those images. From any point in the house, the stone and mortar fireplace was a visible, dramatic focal point. Books—all kinds of books—well used and well read lined shelves built into every conceivable nook and cranny. Vibrantly colored woven rugs lay scattered across the polished pine floors. A pronounced Native American theme influenced stunning prints of everything from wildlife to wild horses and a way of life long over but never forgotten. At least not by this man.

His presence seemed to fill every inch of breathing space, as daylight reluctantly gave way to dusk, and shadows danced like ghosts on the walls. Like the shadows, her gaze danced again from the fire to Abel Greene.

His jaw was square and strong, yet his face was saved from being savagely severe by the warm bronze tint of his skin and the generous width of his mouth. Even tensed into a tight, grim line, that mouth spoke to what she chose to believe was irritation, not anger. If he'd been truly angry, they wouldn't be warming up by his fire right now. If he'd been truly angry, he would have sent them away.

Annoyed, definitely. Unsettled, without a doubt. But now that her panic had subsided her unfortunate outburst of anger was spent, her deepest, strongest impressions were of a man who protected not only what was his, but *who* he was and *what* he was.

She shivered when those eyes, as black as a cold, deep cave, cut to hers and caught her staring at the long, scythe-shaped scar that ran from his right temple down to his jawline. Embarrassed, but no less intrigued, she refused to look away.

By the time they finally broke eye contact, ripples of awareness were coursing through her body, warming the chill that had settled bone deep. There were so many unknowns here. It wasn't that she was helpless. She knew how to take care of herself or she wouldn't have risked coming. Yet she was a small woman, and Mark, for all his tough-thug posturing, was just a boy. They were alone with a man who could use all that strength, all that power against them. He already had. Yet, she reminded herself, he hadn't hurt them. Not even when she'd provoked him.

She'd always relied on her instincts. She counted on them as they cautiously suggested there was a decency in him that would outdistance any threat. They were safe with this man. This man who would be her husband.

Husband. A sensation similar to cresting a hill on a roller coaster before plummeting down the other side flipped her stomach upside down.

Husband. The word caught like a sharp needle on a scratched record.

Mail-order brides had gone out with the gold rush and

pantaloons, yet here she was, setting back the feminist movement by a hundred years. That and the concept of good sense. It wasn't that she'd come into this completely blind. She had given some thought to caution. When she'd finally come to terms with the fact that answering his ad was her only remaining option, she'd checked the character reference the ad had offered. She'd been enthusiastically assured that Abel Greene was the equivalent of saint, savior and salvation. Someone out there thought he walked on water. It had been good enough for her.

She'd answered the ad. She'd given up on any correlation between love and marriage long ago, anyway. Just as she'd given up on the American Dream. She didn't want Mark to give up, though. She wanted him to have a chance. This business arrangement of a marriage would provide it.

Right now, however, business had little to do with her awareness of Abel Greene as a man...and the resulting awareness of herself as a woman. She hadn't counted on that. She hadn't been counting on anything but getting out of the city.

Settling deeper into the sofa, she reflected on the "sell job" she'd received when she'd called the reference listed in his ad. The endorsement she'd been given had been a little too enthusiastic to be taken at face value. "Owned his own business," they'd said. "Stable," they'd said. While their optimism hadn't been guarded, their details had.

She had the details now—at least the physical ones.

Never, in her wildest dreams, had she anticipated tall, dark and dangerous. And never had she come up with a game plan for dealing with a man who offered what this one did in the sex appeal department—or of how lacking she was in that area.

She was a plain Jane. Her short, shaggy hair, at its descriptive best, could be summed up as brown. Not sable, not chestnut, not any of those pretty, poetic synonyms, just brown. Statuesque? Hardly. She was shorter than her gangly fifteen-year-old brother by six inches but slim enough in the hips that she could wear his jeans if she rolled up the pant legs.

Mark drew the line at letting her wear his T-shirts though.

"I don't want you putting bumps in them," he'd grumble, making her grin.

It was true, she did have bumps, but they were just your garden variety B-cup bumps. Again, nothing to write home about. Other than her green eyes, which people seemed to find unusual, she was a blank white page compared to the canvas of rich, vivid color that was Abel Greene.

Tough, she thought, with the same stubbornness that had gotten her this far. He'd taken the same risks she had when he'd run that ad. For better or worse—Mark possibly being the "worse" part—she was going to make sure he saw this through. She had no choice. She'd closed the book on all options but one when she'd left L.A.—and that one option was glaring at her as if she'd arrived by space capsule.

Huddling deeper into the blanket, she comforted herself with the knowledge that even though Green's welcome was cool and grudging, the cabin was blissfully warm and welcoming.

True to form, Mark was still a brooding, angry presence. He sat on the far end of the sofa, fiddling with his boom box, which had been damaged when he'd thrown it at the wolf.

The wolf. Mackenzie shivered and wrapped her hands tighter around her coffee mug. Flinching when her sore knuckle screamed in protest, she stared uneasily at where the wolf in question was curled up on a braided rag rug by the fire.

This, she hadn't been prepared for.

"You live with a wolf," she blurted out into a silence

that emphasized how badly disbelieving she found her conclusion. It also told her she didn't have as solid a grip on her composure as she'd hoped.

Greene handed her another blanket then added more wood to the fire. "Nashata is only half wolf."

"Only half wolf," she mused, considering his stoic response. "Well. I feel much better knowing that. Does that mean he'll only take off half of my leg when he decides he doesn't want to share the fire anymore?"

Some women cried when they were nervous. Some women clammed up. Unfortunately, she got mouthy. Oneliners were her specialty. As a defense mechanism, it lacked both tact and wisdom. Knowledge of that pitfall wasn't enough to take the edge off. Neither was it enough to shut her up.

She couldn't stop herself from sniping now. She was too tired. Her knuckle hurt. Her thawing fingers and toes burned as life returned to her frozen digits. Her stomach growled, complaining that the greasy donut she'd fed it at seven-thirty that morning had long ago lost its miserly attempt at appeasing her hunger.

Aware of the quiet that had settled, she lifted her gaze to his.

"What?" she demanded defensively.

"She," he said, as if repeating a point he was trying to make.

When her frown relayed she wasn't connecting, he tried again. "Nashata...she's female."

"Oh. Better and better. Maybe I can appeal to her on a woman-to-woman basis to eat her dog chow tonight instead of us."

Greene's impossibly broad shoulders rose with a very huge, very weary breath. "You don't have to be afraid of Nashata."

"Excuse me," she snapped, wishing she hadn't, wishing

everything hadn't set her on such a sharp edge. She jerked the blankets tighter around her shoulders. "It's just that in my experience, low feral growls and bared teeth don't generally say 'nice doggie' to me."

Just like your nasty scowls don't exactly spell out happily ever after, she thought glumly.

Only the possibility that his response would be "So leave," kept her from voicing those thoughts. As unsettling as the idea of actually marrying this sullen, beautiful man was, even more frightening was the thought that he might send them away.

When she braved another look at him, he was still staring, but his expression had shifted from irritation to thoughtful contemplation. And the softness of his voice when he spoke sparked a flicker of hope.

"She was only protecting her property." His gaze, but not his attention, drifted to the dog before returning to her. "Now that she knows I've accepted you, she has, too."

Mackenzie eyed the wolf-dog as she made an amazingly human-sounding groan and stretched out full-length on the rug.

She had to admit that here, in the warmth of the cabin, lazy and relaxed by the fire, the animal did look harmless. Overpowering that conclusion, however, was Greene's use of the word *accepted* in reference to her. It eased her mind marginally. Acceptance was what she needed.

She settled herself down and offered him a peacemaking smile. "Now that you mention it, she does look a little too well fed to want anything as tough as the two of us for a meal."

She'd stopped hoping for a return smile. With good reason. It wasn't going to happen.

"She's two days away from whelping."

"Whelping?" She sent a concerned look to the dog, then back to Greene. "As in…having puppies?"

He nodded, then knelt beside the dog and ran his hand over her back.

No wonder he'd looked so angry when they'd run into him. They'd thrown things at his pregnant dog. The boom box had narrowly missed making a direct hit.

Clutching the blankets around her, Mackenzie leaned forward and peeked worriedly over his shoulder. "Is she all right?"

"I didn't hurt his damn dog," Mark snapped.

Up until now he'd been ignoring them in martyred silence. He threw a sullen, resentful look at the dog before turning his anger on Greene.

"Because of that mutt, my box is ruined."

"Mark," Mackenzie cautioned, knowing he only pretended disdain for the dog's condition. She remembered him as a little boy who used to sneak stray cats into their apartment and feed them milk.

"Don't 'Mark' me!" he shouted above the din of quiet his outburst prompted. "Don't even talk to me!"

Shoving the broken radio to the floor, he shot off the sofa and stalked to the window. Her tough, macho, little brother hadn't turned his back soon enough, though. Mackenzie caught the shine of moisture crowding his thick-lashed eyes. Her heart ached for him even as he railed at her.

"I hate this!" he snarled between clenched teeth. "Why did you make me come here? It's the middle of freaking nowhere! You take me away from everything I know to...to what?" He spun around and glared at Abel then Nashata. "Mad Max and a knocked-up wolf?"

Glaring at Mackenzie, he muttered a gutter-bred expletive. "The radio was my only connection with civilization, and now I don't even have that!"

Snagging his jacket from the coatrack by the door, he

shoved his feet into his army boots and slammed out of the cabin into the storm.

She was too tired to do anything but watch him go. Watch and wonder if she could ever heal the huge, festering hurts inside his thin, gangly body. And to wonder how, with Mark as a selling point, she was going to convince Abel Greene that this particular "two-fer" was a bargain he just couldn't pass up.

Abel stared at the door long after the boy had slammed it behind him. Reluctantly he let his gaze swing to Mackenzie Kincaid where she sat huddled on his sofa. The kid's outburst had hurt her.

It wasn't his problem, he reminded himself coldly. At any rate, he sure as hell didn't want it to be. Just like he didn't want to be aware that the woman who'd been gutsy enough to find her way through a snowstorm, then lay into him with a wicked roundhouse punch, had lost her fire when the kid had stalked out.

He brought his hand to his jaw. It still throbbed from the impact of her small fist. And his mind was still railing at him for putting himself, and them, in this position.

He damned his friend J. D. Hazzard for his stupid idea. Then the U.S. mail that evidently hadn't delivered his letter calling things off. Ultimately, though, he had no one to blame but himself. J.D. may have been the button pusher, and the whiskey the two of them had consumed that one fateful night might have lowered his guard, but he was the one who'd knuckled under. He'd submitted to a weakness, and now he had to deal with it.

They couldn't stay, of course. But neither could they go. Not tonight, at any rate. Not in this storm. Tomorrow, at first light, he'd lay it all out for her. He was sorry she'd come all this way. It wasn't his fault she hadn't gotten his letter calling the arrangement off. She'd either accept it or she wouldn't. Either way he was going to drive them the thirty miles to Bordertown and put them on the first bus back to L.A.

An uncomfortable quiet had settled over the cabin. He'd intended to ignore her, yet when she rose on shaking legs, bent on going after the boy, he reacted.

"He'll be all right," he said when her eyes—as green and fresh as the forest in spring, yet as old as a hundred cold winters—met his.

"He could freeze out there."

Her voice was a sandpapery whisper of concern, as weary as the look in her eyes. She was too young to have eyes that old. And she was too tired to succeed in hiding her vulnerability with a smart mouth and a lift of that stubborn chin.

He didn't much like that he'd let her get to him, but it didn't stop him from trying to reassure her. "He'll be back long before it comes to that."

She looked toward the door again. "He could get lost."

"He's too smart for that, too. He'll be all right," he repeated with more gentleness than he'd thought he had in him. "Let him walk it out."

She shook her head, a small, tired smile barely tipping the corners of her mouth. "There aren't enough miles between here and L.A. for Mark to walk off all the anger inside him."

"Then why the hell did you bring him here?"

The question burst out before he could stop it. This was a road he didn't want to travel. He didn't want to know why they were here. He didn't want to know anything about her—until she raised her head and those green eyes of hers touched him again.

"Maybe for the same reasons you ran the ad."

She had deadly insight. He'd concluded that it had been despair that had sent her here, and she'd just told him she knew it had been his own desperation that had initiated the ad.

He clenched his jaw, wanting to deny that she—that anyone—could so easily understand that part of him. He liked even less that he understood her motives. She may have a smart mouth, but those eyes held secrets and sorrow.

She was running from something. He was certain of it. Just like he was certain he didn't want to know what it was. Ignorance might not necessarily be bliss, but it went a long way to help maintain distance. And distance was the only good thing that could come between them.

When she weaved on her feet and grasped the back of the sofa to regain her balance, he muttered a curse.

"Would you mind if we finished this conversation sitting down?"

He'd been so absorbed in denying what she was doing to him, he'd looked past the obvious. She was exhausted. She'd been close to frozen when he'd found her.

"Sit," he ordered gruffly. "You need food."

And he needed space. And time to decide what he was going to do about her.

His mood blackened along with his scowl. A moment ago he'd known exactly what he was going to do. He was going to send her back to L.A.

But that had been a moment ago. Before he'd let himself look into her eyes and glimpse a soul that too closely mirrored his own.

He watched her from the kitchen as he heated thick stew, and refused to be impressed with her grit. She could have been—should have been—wailing about everything from the cold to his surly company. But she didn't say a word. She just curled her shivering limbs into a ball and wrapped herself up in his blankets.

For lack of anything better to do, he damned J. D. Hazzard again. Ever since he'd married Maggie Adams, J.D. had been trying to come up with a way to get him paired up with a woman.

"So you can share the experience," J.D. had said. He regularly badgered Abel when he called from Minneapolis, where he and Maggie lived part of the time to be close to J.D.'s air-freight business and Maggie's new photography studio.

"Marrying Maggie was the best thing that ever happened to me," J.D. assured Abel whenever he returned to the lake, his face splitting with that candy-eating grin he got whenever he looked at his wife.

That road went both ways. Marrying J.D. was the best thing that had ever happened to Maggie, too. When Abel had stumbled onto her in the little cabin in the next bay last spring, she'd reminded him of a deer caught in a hunter's spotlight. She'd been afraid of her own shadow, hiding out alone. When J.D. had literally dropped out of the sky in his float plane, he'd fixed whatever was wrong with Maggie's life.

It was damn lucky for Hazzard that he had. Maggie was one of the few people on the lake Abel called friend. J.D. fell in that category now too, after the battle they'd waged against a nasty bunch of poachers last year.

But, friendship notwithstanding, if J. D. Hazzard were within grinning distance right now, Abel would cheerfully knock his pretty-boy blond block off for getting him into this situation.

He had little to give a woman, nothing to give a woman like her. Nothing good, anyway. No woman—not even one foolish enough to answer that ad—deserved the grief that tying herself up with him would bring.

She may be gutsy. The fact that she was here was proof of that. But despite the wisdom in her eyes, he could tell she was an innocent. Innocence deserved reward, not punishment. He wouldn't—no matter how tempting—drag her down with him. And he couldn't, no matter what she thought, solve the problem that had made her run to him.

When the stew was hot, he took her a bowl. She thanked him, but merely played with it while casting worried glances toward the door.

He'd decided, even before she'd told him, that the boy was her brother. The blood relationship was evident. It wasn't just the unusual green of their eyes or the cinnamon brown of their hair. The boy's features, though more sharply drawn in the ragged gauntness of gender and youth, mirrored hers.

He didn't want to, but he watched her while she finally began to eat. Her features, like her size, were understated. Her nose was upturned just enough to give her a waifish, elfin look, her bone structure sufficiently refined to lend elegance. She was small and...birdlike, he finally decided, wondering where that analogy had come from. Maybe it was the flighty way she moved. Maybe it was that she appeared so fragile yet was so obviously resilient.

His growing fascination with her eyes and the rosy glow of her winter-bitten cheeks irritated him. And despite his determination to send her on her way in the morning, his increasing speculation about the soft curves rounding out her sweatsuit couldn't be ignored.

He'd become unaccountably aware of her presence. He didn't want to analyze why, but there was a subtle difference in the feel of the cabin with her in it. Dark, empty shadows seemed full of light and space. Hard, sharp edges felt somehow softer—and he was soft in the head for letting his thoughts stray in that direction.

"If he's not back in another ten minutes, I'll go find him," he said, as much to break the silence as to get his mind out of places it had no business going.

His offer seemed to satisfy her.

Satisfaction, however, was a far cry from what he felt as he watched her.

She was asleep when the boy came back ten minutes later. The scent of horse and hay followed him in the back door telling Abel he'd found the stable and the pair of black Belgian mares inside. The horses' calming nature and the harsh winter night had wrestled the fight out of the kid. He was as dead on his feet as his sister.

Abel didn't wake her. He left her curled up on the sofa, and in a silence that matched the boy's, he fed him, showed him to the bathroom, then shoved a sleeping bag and pillow into his arms and pointed in the direction of the loft.

Too exhausted to do more than climb the stairs, the boy crawled into the bag and fell immediately asleep.

For Abel, however, sleep was a long time coming.

He sat in the chair across from the sofa, an elbow propped on the armrest, his chin on his fist, his eyes on Mackenzie Kincaid.

She stirred. And so did his sex, as her scent—a sweet, exotic blend of winter and summer and the softness of woman—reminded him what was missing from his life.

It had been a long time since he'd been with a woman. Even at that, the pull of desire that tugged deep and low was too strong. The catalyst was far too weak.

Abstinence notwithstanding, his past was littered with memories of far more alluring women. Mackenzie was a woman, yes, but a small, untidy package of disheveled brown hair, green urchin eyes and boyishly slim limbs. A pretty, colorful little bird, like those who visited his feeders.

A siren she was not. But still an arresting, provocative presence.

An innocent, he reminded himself, and he knew he should go to bed.

Yet he sat there long into the night and watched her sleep.

Three

"Crimson Falls to Greene's Point. Come in Greene's Point. Hey, Abel, it's Casey. How's our little chief doing? Is she a momma yet? Over."

The crackle of static, a shrill whine that sounded like feedback from a microphone and a muffled, feminine voice infiltrated Mackenzie's sleep-drugged fog.

She tugged the blanket over her head and snuggled deeper into the pillow, bent on ignoring it.

"Come on, Abel. Answer me. Mom's worried about how you're weathering the storm over there and I'm worried about Nashata. Over."

Mackenzie pried one eye open. Okay. So she wasn't going to be able to ignore it, she realized when the voice, sounding like that of a young girl, spoke again, more persistent this time.

Unfolding slowly to accommodate the deep ache in every joint, she rose to a sitting position. She finger-combed her short hair, winced at the stiffness in her right hand and cast a squinty look around for the source of the noise. In the process, she made a major discovery.

"We're not in Kansas anymore, Toto," she murmured, and reacclimated herself to the fact that California was a couple thousand miles away and she'd just spent the night on a sofa in a cabin belonging to a man she didn't know but was about to marry. And that he had a granite jaw, she reflected, wincing when she flexed her sore knuckle.

"That's life in the fast lane," she mumbled around a huge yawn, then opened her eyes fully.

"Abel are you there? Over." The voice was pretty and profoundly feminine but was beginning to sound downright pouty as it drifted over the airwaves.

At least Mackenzie assumed it was airwaves. Her assumption was confirmed when she followed the sound of the disembodied voice to a doorway tucked beneath the loft stairs.

The door stood open, revealing a small room that had all the earmarks of an office. Two four-drawer file cabinets and a wall of shelves overflowing with books, magazines, loose papers and assorted sketches stood against one wall.

Strategically placed, where the light from a set of casement windows gave the best advantage, was a draftsman's desk. An old pine desk, nestled in the opposite corner, held a computer, phone, fax and what she assumed was a short-wave radio.

While this was all very interesting, the biggest surprise was that Mark was sitting at that desk, studying the radio while the wolf dog lay on the floor at his bare feet.

"Abel, come on. Answer me, will you? Over."

Mackenzie was about to investigate the radio when Mark picked a switch, flipped it and groused into the microphone. "He ain't here."

She groaned inwardly at his surly delivery. Before she

could admonish him, the anonymous voice came back on the air.

"Is this Abel Greene's base? Over."

"Well, it ain't Mick Jagger's."

Mackenzie closed her eyes and shook her head, but something made her hang back in the doorway.

A protracted silence followed before the girl tried again. "Who are you...and where's Abel? Over."

"Who are *you* and how'm I supposed to know where he is?"

"Well you don't have to be so rude," she snapped right back. "Over."

"And you don't have to be so snotty. You woke me up, ya know."

"Well, *excuuuuuse* me. Over."

Good for you, Mackenzie thought with a grin. And what's this? Mark's back was to her, but he turned his head enough that she caught the whisper of a cynical smile tip up one corner of his mouth. Her best guess was that Mark was enjoying the fact that the girl on the other end could give back as good as she got.

"So, what'd you say your name was, sweet thing?"

From her spot in the doorway, Mackenzie rolled her eyes. Testosterone had taken over. Every mother's living nightmare, or in this case, every sister's living nightmare could be blamed on that one, obnoxious chemical.

"Wouldn't you like to know. Over," came back the flinty but flirty reply.

"Not necessarily. But it beats sitting here watching this stupid dog slobber on my feet."

"Nashata? Is Nashata with you? Over."

"Yeah," Mark drawled, trying to sound disgusted but not quite pulling it off. "The mutt's here."

"Is she all right? Did she have her puppies yet? Over."

The girl's voice had risen with anxiety. Amazingly, Mark

responded to it—with as little empathy as possible, but with empathy, just the same.

"She's fine," he said, and unaware that he was being watched, he reached down and stroked the wolf dog's head.

Mackenzie brought her hand to her throat where her heart had suddenly lodged. And for once, when she looked at her brother, the tears that stung her eyes weren't prompted by worry, frustration or fear. The openly affectionate gesture lit a small flame of hope inside her.

"And no," he continued, back in his tough punk role, "she ain't had any little mutts yet. What's it to you, anyway?"

"You are really a creep, you know that? Over."

"And you're really a bore."

Mackenzie sighed. So much for pleasant interaction with the locals.

While he'd never admit it, Mark was enjoying this little airwave sparring. When the girl didn't respond, she sensed disappointment in the sudden droop of his shoulders.

"What's the matter?" he said, attempting to lure her back on the air. "Did I scare you off, little girl?"

"Who am I speaking to please?"

Uh-oh. A new voice had joined the discussion. This one, while ringing with the same pleasant tones as the girl's, was the mature voice of a woman. Mackenzie bolted away from the door and grabbed the mike before Mark had a chance to alienate yet one more unknown person.

"Which switch?" she asked Mark, who shot her a surprised look before shrugging, flipping a lever and stalking out of the room, the wolf dog at his heels.

"Good morning," Mackenzie said, a little hesitant as she tried to smooth things over. "I'm Mackenzie Kincaid, and that charming young man who just offended that sweet young lady is my little brother. I'm sorry he was so rude. He's...he's been under a bit of a strain the past few days."

Strain, she thought with a grim press of her lips. That benign summation was the understatement of the decade.

"Well, hi, Mackenzie. I'm Scarlett Morgan and the pouty little prima donna he was offending is my daughter, Casey. And don't worry about it. We don't have to be proud of how they sometimes act. We just have to bear it. Over."

Settling into the chair Mark had vacated, Mackenzie relaxed a little, liking this woman and her tolerance, sight unseen. "Amen to that."

"So, Mackenzie, is Abel around? Over."

She sensed even before he leaned over her that Abel was definitely around.

A watershed of sensations swamped her as she looked up over her shoulder and saw him standing there. His size was every bit as imposing as she remembered from last night. And he was still every bit as beautiful.

His hair, which he'd tied at his nape, trailed over one shoulder, dragging across the desktop as he leaned toward the radio. His chest brushed her back in the process. It was just a brief touch, yet a ripple of awareness shimmered down her spine.

He was scented of winter-crisp air and warm cedar smoke, telling her he'd just come in from outside and had made a stop to stoke the fire before discovering her in his office. And she was far too aware of the heat and strength of his body just a deep breath away from touching her again.

When his fingers brushed hers as he took the mike from her hand, a jolt like an electric shock sizzled through her blood. She bolted out of the chair and backed a few feet away, hugging her hand, still warm and tingling from his touch, to her breast.

Unable to look away, she watched him in profile as he ignored her and spoke into the mike.

"Morning, Scarlett. How are things over at Crimson Falls? You holding up okay in this storm? Over."

Another sensation slammed through her chest at his words. Not his words so much as at his tone of voice. The sensation was jealousy. Even though it caught her off guard, even though it made no sense, she didn't pretend to mistake it for anything other than what it was.

Those few words, spoken to a faceless woman, held tender concern, an intimate, affectionate regard. After hearing little but curt, hard-edged tones from him yesterday, it was like comparing sandpaper to velvet, reminding her how precarious their position here was.

"We're fine, Abel. This storm's a doozy, isn't it? I don't believe I've ever seen snow set in this fast and deep so early in the season. Over."

"Looks like we're in for a long winter," he said, casting a glance out the window. "So, are you going to be able to handle it? Over."

"No problem. We've got plenty of wood. I just stocked up on groceries, and even though the phones are out, as long as the radio works, we won't go stir crazy up here. Over."

"I'll hear from you if you need anything. Over."

It wasn't a question as much as it was a command. Clearly he cared about this woman and her daughter. And evidently, there wasn't any other man in their life to take care of them.

"You know we will. What about things there? Casey says Nashata is still holding out on us. Over."

"Won't be much longer now. Tell her not to worry. She's still got first pick of the litter. I'll radio just as soon as I can after the big event. Over."

"And what about you, Abel? Are you holding out on us too? Is Mackenzie the, ah, *guest* J.D. told me you were expecting?"

Listening in silence to the conversation, Mackenzie quickly added two and two and came up with a colossal six. Scarlett Morgan could only be referring to J. D. Hazzard. It was J.D. and his wife, Maggie Hazzard, who had been listed as references in Abel's ad. Scarlett's mention of J.D implied that she was a friend of his, too. Based on the familiarity and the affectionately curious quality of her question, it also suggested Scarlett knew about the mail-order bride business.

Mackenzie held her breath, waiting for Abel's reply.

"J. D. Hazzard's got a big mouth," he muttered.

"And a big heart," Scarlett reminded him with a laugh. "I swear, that man is not going to be happy until he sees us both married and—"

"Miss Kincaid and her brother got caught in the storm," he cut in, dodging any further discussion about marriage. "It seems Mother Nature is indiscriminate about who she strands and where. Over."

Mackenzie's heart, along with her hopes, sank a little lower. He was deliberately letting Scarlett think she and Mark were accidents of the storm and nothing more. He obviously didn't want Scarlett to know the significance of Mackenzie's presence. Which made her even more uneasy about what he planned to do about them.

Scarlett was evidently disappointed, too. After a long pause she came back on the air. "Oh. Well. I was hoping that maybe...well...you know."

Abel hit the switch. "Is there anything else I can do for you, Scarlett? Over."

It didn't take a degree in advanced psychology to figure out that Abel wanted to close this conversation. Scarlett took the hint.

"No," she said carefully. "As I said, we're fine. Maybe we can do something for you, though. You're not exactly set up for unexpected company over there. Would you like to bring Miss Kincaid and her brother over to the hotel? We can put them up here at Crimson Falls until the storm lifts. Over.''

Here it comes, she thought. His chance to get rid of them.

''Not an option,'' he quickly said, surprising her. ''Until this bad boy blows itself out, no one's going anywhere. You make damn sure you stay put, too. Don't go outside if you don't have to. And don't let Casey even think about firing up the snowmobile until the snow stops and the wind dies down. She'd get lost so fast in this mess she'd freeze to death before anyone found her. Over.''

Soft laughter rang over the air. ''There you go, sounding just like J.D. He's already radioed. By the way—did you know he and Maggie are at their cabin? They drove up from the Cities to spend a long weekend. Got here just before the storm hit. Anyway, he's already checked on us. I'll tell you the same thing I told him—we don't need any brother hens clucking over us. Casey and I can take care of ourselves. Over.''

''Just see to it that you do. Over.''

''Mackenzie,'' Scarlett continued, addressing her instead of Abel, ''if you had to get stranded in a snowstorm, you couldn't pick a better man to rescue you than Abel. He'll take good care of you. Over.''

With a reluctant scowl and a long look, Abel handed her the mike, taking great care this time to avoid touching her hand.

''Thanks, Scarlett,'' she said hesitantly. ''I'll try to remember that.''

''And don't let his big bad wolf routine intimidate you. It's all an act. Over.''

''Thanks again,'' she said, and unable to resist she added, ''I'll keep that in mind the next time he bares his teeth.''

Scarlett laughed again. ''Atta girl. Something tells me

you can handle yourself just fine with him. Where are you from by the way? Over."

"California" popped out before she thought about it. The look Abel gave her made her wish she hadn't said it.

"California?" More than polite curiosity colored Scarlett's surprised response. A short pause followed. "Abel...I thought J.D. said—"

Before she could finish, he commandeered the mike again. "Time to sign off. I don't want to tie up the airwaves, in case someone needs help. Let me hear from you if you need anything. Over and out."

With a flip of the switch, he broke the connection and backed away from the desk. He moved so quickly Mackenzie felt the air stir like a cool breeze around her. She could almost picture Scarlett on the other end of the line, frowning at the sudden silence and Abel's puzzling abruptness.

"Why do I feel like I'm the family secret no one wants to talk about?" she mumbled with a final glance at the radio. And why was she getting the impression that in addition to J.D. and Maggie Hazzard, Scarlett Morgan would like to see Abel Greene join the ranks of the happily-ever-after crowd?

She filed the bit of information away. It could come in handy if push came to shove and he balked at keeping the bargain. The Hazzards and Scarlett Morgan might prove to be just the allies she needed.

It won't come to that, she told herself as she turned to leave the room—and ran smack into the solid wall of Abel Greene's chest.

His hands shot out to steady her, but not before she'd lost her balance and landed flush against him. Everything registered at once. The feel of those huge hands cupping her upper arms. The heat of him. His dark, woodsy scent.

A powerful strength countered by an innate gentleness. The unsteady, heavy pounding of his heart against her breasts.

She drew a deep breath. When her own heart rate evened out, she looked up at his face, not knowing what to expect.

His eyes were closed, his jaw clenched. And the hands that held her both steady and captive, tightened before they loosened and he set her away.

"We have to talk."

His voice sounded smoky and rough as he opened his eyes and looked not at her but over the top of her head.

Slowly she nodded. Carefully she agreed. "You're right. We do. But is there a chance I could shower first? I need to work a little stiffness out of my bones, and a shower might just do the trick."

A glazed look came over his eyes, and in the moment they met hers she swore he was picturing her in the shower and considering joining her there.

An instant later his hard scowl was firmly back in place. He backed away. "Fine. Shower. Towels are in the cabinet by the sink."

Then he turned on his heel and hotfooted it out of the room.

He'd been in tight spots in his life, both before and after he'd opted out of the marines ten years ago. He'd missed the Gulf War, but not the drug war, first as an undercover cop and then later as he'd scrambled for his life for the "Company." Later still, his belly full of being used, and knowing he, too, was dispensable to the CIA, he'd freelanced for any country who'd had need of his services and the cash to pay for them. It had still been his neck on the line, but calling his own shots ensured he had a fighting chance.

But never, in all those dark, ugly experiences, had he felt

as defenseless as he had two minutes ago facing one small green-eyed woman.

He jabbed at the fire with a poker, thinking that war, whether fought on a battlefield or on back streets, seedy bars or jungle undergrowth, was never personal. War was a job. Someone tried to kill you. You tried not to let them. What he'd felt when he'd held Mackenzie Kincaid in his arms with those soulful eyes trained on his was as personal as it got.

Last night he'd had one hell of a personal struggle. After the boy had settled down in the loft, he'd sat by the fire, gauging the strength of the wind and the force of the front as ice-laced snow peppered the window panes. He'd watched, not entirely surprised, when Nashata rose from her nest by the fire, tiptoed with a soft click of her toenails up the loft stairs and settled with a whisper of goose down on the sleeping bag by the boy.

Nashata, too, had sensed the need in the troubled kid. Her reaction had been instinctive, as elemental as that of a kindred soul and less removed from human emotion than most humans would feel comfortable admitting.

The boy had stirred in surprise, then in his state of fatigue, had let down his guard and welcomed Nashata's warmth and company. Abel understood the boy. That knowledge ate at him. He didn't know the reason for his anger, but he recognized the intensity of it. He'd had the same rage at Mark's age—didn't feel that distanced from it even now. Was close enough to it, in fact, that he felt a keen and unwelcome sense of empathy for both the boy and the woman.

The woman. When he'd finally gone to bed he'd tried to convince himself he didn't like having his privacy invaded. Told himself it was a curse not a blessing, knowing that somewhere in this cabin, a human heartbeat other than his own pulsed softly. A body other than his own shared space and warmth and silence.

The problem was that her presence in his home had intensified his feelings of loss—and of how alone he'd felt the night he'd broken down and let J.D. place that ad.

He set the poker in the stand, his thoughts returning against his will to Mackenzie Kincaid. To her softness, her slim curves, to the puzzle that had sent her to him. As he had last night, he found himself stacking common sense against uncommon need and wondering if, despite her troubled kid brother and the threat hanging over his business, he'd have the sense to send her back to L.A.

He considered his life to date: a past littered with regrets, a future promising more of the same. He was thirty-five years old. He'd either been alone or felt alone for every one of them. That he'd always been and would always be an outsider was a truth he'd accepted when he'd left the lake all those years ago as an angry and rebellious eighteen-year-old. He'd never intended to come back. Only when he'd run out of options had he returned. And only when the loneliness had gotten a choke hold, had he let himself be duped into placing that damned ad.

"What about you, green eyes?" he murmured, searching the fire and seeing those young-old eyes that captivated him. "Is that why you're here? Have you run out of options, too?"

He reminded himself he couldn't afford to invest in someone else's misery. He especially couldn't use it to temper his own. No matter how tempting she was.

Besides, wisdom dictated that he send her away. He had to get her out of here for her own good. If his suspicions played out and the last of his business mishaps—a fire at his main storage shed just last week—wasn't an accident, that meant it had been deliberately set. He didn't want to believe it, but it was a possibility, and he couldn't involve her or her brother in a potentially dangerous situation.

If someone wanted him gone—and he had a pretty good idea who that someone might be—that someone was in for a surprise.

Abel Greene had reset his roots. He wasn't going anywhere. And if he did have a problem, he'd deal with it the same way he had every other problem in his life. Alone.

He'd had it all in perspective when he'd come in from taking care of the horses this morning—and then he'd run into Mackenzie Kincaid in his office.

She'd looked sleep mussed and dewy soft and so very touchable. All the speculations he'd wrestled with through the night—the feel of her, the softness of flesh over fragile bones, the heat and scent of woman—were speculation no more.

His hands were still shaking from holding her. Lower in his body, deep in his groin, an ache, hot and demanding had begun to intensify and burn at the memory of the soft brush of her thighs against his legs, the cushion of her breasts pulsing against his chest.

"That's what you get, Greene," he muttered under his breath as he stalked out of the living room and headed for the kitchen.

"You hold up out here for five years like a damn hermit and then you're surprised when a body with breasts knocks you for a loop."

He jerked open a cupboard, grabbed the coffee can off the top shelf and slammed around making a fresh pot.

Then he tried to get a grip. Bracing his hands wide on the counter, he dropped his head between his hunched shoulders and dragged in a deep, controlling breath.

"She can really piss a guy off, huh?"

He spun around like he'd been shot.

Sitting at the table, digging into a bowl of cereal, sat the kid. From the look on his face, Abel surmised he'd heard every muttered word.

He scrubbed a hand over his jaw. "I'm not angry at your sister."

The boy shrugged. "Whatever." Then a nasty smirk curled his upper lip. "So…are you gonna do her?"

Anger exploded inside Abel like a bomb. He skirted the table in two strides, grabbed the boy's shirt in one fist and jerked him nose to nose before he had a chance to run for cover.

"Look, you little punk. I don't know what's eating you, but a man doesn't bad-mouth a woman because his nose is out of joint. Don't ever make reference to your sister in that tone or that way again. Understood?"

Eyes bulging, face red, hands clasped in a death grip around Abel's wrist, Mark nodded. Once. Then again, in a series of rapid, jerky movements.

Slowly Abel let him go. Slower still, aware that the boy was watching his every move in wary silence, he backed away. Without breaking eye contact, he reached behind him to the counter where he'd left the boom box after he'd repaired it earlier this morning.

Without a word, he set it in front of him.

Unsure of what he was supposed to do with it, the boy stared first at the box then at Abel.

"Don't give me a reason to break it."

Humbled, yet too proud to give in to humiliation and too pleased by the prospect of listening to his precious radio, the boy nodded. "No, sir." Then he stood, pushing back his chair and picked up the radio.

"The dirty dishes go in the sink," Abel said, pouring himself a cup of coffee.

At the least he'd expected a belligerent scowl. At the most, a suggestion to stick it. Instead Mark picked up his bowl and spoon and walked them to the sink. When he returned to the table for his radio, he hesitated, then swallowing hard, faced Abel again. "Thanks," he croaked.

Abel regarded him over his coffee cup, then accepted the unexpected thanks with a nod.

With Nashata at his side, and the boom box under his arm, Mark headed for the loft. Abel was standing there watching them go when he realized he had an audience.

He turned his head and found Mackenzie standing in the doorway. She looked like an untidy elf. She didn't look like a woman who would accelerate a man's heartbeat and heat his blood. Yet she did—in spades.

Jaw clenched, he took in her drab, gray sweats, her hair tousled and shaggy, her green eyes full and glistening. The look on her face nearly destroyed him. It held too much. Too much respect. Too much gratitude. Too much hope.

"Thank you," she said softly. "Thank you for setting him straight."

Then, hugging a towel to her breast, she turned toward the bathroom, walked down the hall and shut the door behind her.

Four

He might have known she'd get the wrong idea. He might have known she'd take the dressing down he'd given the boy as a sign that he cared. Caring had nothing to do with it. Emotions long buried and seldom addressed had nothing to do with it. He hadn't hurt for the boy, hadn't speculated at his source of conflict, hadn't answered a need to set him back on course.

Like hell he hadn't—but he'd be damned if he'd let her think it made any difference. He scrubbed a hand across his jaw and set his mind to the task. She'd had her rest. And as soon as she had her shower, she was going to get the facts.

When she emerged from the bathroom a few minutes later dressed in tight old jeans and a bulky red sweater, he was ready to lay things out for her without preamble. He could have pulled it off, too, if the look of her hadn't blown his plans all to hell.

She held him spellbound, speechless and...hungry, he admitted, as she again managed to tap his sexual urges that were out of place and out of time. Hungry for the softness she possessed, which had been missing so long from his life. Hungry for the womanly scents she brought with her—strawberries and cream and spring rain—as the steam from her shower rolled out of the bathroom in her wake. Hungry for what J.D. had with Maggie and he'd been fool enough to think he could have for himself.

He swore under his breath. Damn her for answering the ad. And damn the insufferable storm. It should have blown itself out by now, but it hadn't let up and didn't show signs of easing up anytime soon. The wind howled around the cabin like a wolf calling the pack home, deepening the drifts, dumping more snow as it screamed across the lake lands.

He was stuck with her until the front moved on. In the meantime, if he was going to get through this, he was going to have to get a grip. And he was going to make it clear that this foolishness about a mail-order marriage wasn't going to happen.

"Sit down," he said stiffly when she shuffled on bare feet into the kitchen.

"Coffee?" he added in a grudging attempt at civility.

Either she didn't catch the sharp edge to his voice, or she chose, for whatever reasons, to ignore it.

"Coffee would be great." She smiled and settled cross-legged into a chair at the table, fluffing her damp hair with a towel.

He poured her a cup, working hard at ignoring all the subtle, provocative jiggling that was taking place under her sweater while she did it.

"Black, right?"

"You got it. Black and bitey, just the way you made it last night."

He set her coffee on the table in front of her, determined to say his peace. But he made a mistake then. He looked at her. He hadn't intended more than a glance, but his gaze snagged on her eyes as she inhaled the scent of the coffee with an exuberant, almost childlike pleasure.

Then he made another mistake. He let his attention linger and drift from the waifish elegance of her bone structure to the wet tangle of short, dark hair softly wisping around her face and finally to the full, lush ripeness of her lips as she brought the cup to her mouth.

"Umm." She closed her eyes and exhaled a sumptuous sigh. "Good. I needed this bad."

He pulled out a chair, his jaw clenched against the picture she made, all comfy and content as a cat and looking sexier than a squirt of a woman like her had a right to. Spinning the chair around backward, he straddled it and crossed his forearms over its back.

"How's your hand," he asked gruffly, noticing, not for the first time, the slight swelling of her knuckle, and wrestling with the guilt that he had been the cause of it.

"About as good as your jaw, I suspect." She grinned sheepishly. "Sorry about that. Sometimes...sometimes I act before I think."

And he never acted before he thought it out thoroughly. That's why it caught him completely off guard when he had to stop himself from returning her smile. The word *infectious* came to mind. She smiled, and it did something to his insides that was totally foreign, undeniably pleasant—and entirely unacceptable.

This chitchat had to stop. It reeked of coziness—and he'd never done *cozy* in his life.

"Look," he said, staring at the steam rising from his cup so he wouldn't be distracted by all that soft feminine warmth nestled across the table from him. "We need to talk about this..."

"Situation?" she suggested, her eyes bright when he paused.

His gaze shot to hers. "Yeah. Situation," he agreed, marginally miffed that she'd not only finished his sentence for him but pinned down the word he'd been searching for.

"When I placed that ad," he began again, shifting uncomfortably in his chair, "there were..." Again he let the line trail off, groping for the right word.

"Circumstances?"

He arched a brow. "Yeah," he said tightly. "There were circumstances. Just like I suspect you might have been experiencing some circumstances of your own when you ran across it."

He waited a beat. When she said nothing, just met his gaze with that fresh, open, green-eyed expectancy, he cleared his throat and continued. "The truth is, I never figured anyone would actually..."

"Answer it?" she supplied, looking helpful.

He set his cup down. Hard. "Do you always finish other people's sentences for them?"

"Sorry." She grinned, looking a little embarrassed but not one bit sorry. "Old habit. *Bad* habit," she amended, pulling a contrite face. "I'll try to control myself."

He closed his eyes, scratched his jaw and told himself he didn't find her or her impertinence refreshing, cute or appealing.

"And I'll try to be direct," he said with businesslike gruffness. "But do I really have to spell this out for you?"

For the first time since she'd sat down, her composure faltered. She swallowed, then averted her gaze to her coffee. "I guess maybe you do."

Her sudden vulnerability unsettled him. The last thing he wanted was for her to see how much. Edgy, uncomfortable, he rose, stalked to the counter and snagged the coffeepot.

"This…your coming here…it never should have happened."

When he turned back to her all the color had drained from her face. "What are you saying?"

He set his jaw and told himself nothing was going to sway him. "I'm saying I never should have placed the ad. And you never should have answered it."

"But you *did*," she pointed out unnecessarily, the tight edge of tension lifting her voice. "And I *did* answer it," she reminded him, also unnecessarily, but with a decided implication that she considered it the overriding issue.

He leaned a hip against the counter, then looked away from the startling intensity of her eyes—and the plea he'd seen in them.

"If you didn't intend to follow through, why did you do it?"

He doubted very much that she'd be mollified if he told her that one night, between a fifth of whiskey that he rarely indulged in and the well-intentioned badgering of J.D. Hazzard, he'd knuckled under to a loneliness that had settled marrow deep. Weakness had never been an option in his life. He hated himself for giving in to it then. He hated admitting to it now, but figured he owed her at least that much.

"Call it a weak moment," he muttered in disgust. "Call it a mistake. Call it whatever you want, but it never should have gone this far."

"But it has."

Though she was as still as the lake on a windless day, the panic in her tone revived his suspicion that she was on the run. And scared. So scared she was going to fight him on this, when she should be relieved as hell that he was letting her off the hook.

"Doesn't this entire concept strike you as insane? Doesn't the idea of answering an ad in a newspaper and agreeing to marry someone you don't know from Adam reek of desperation?''

She was silent for a moment, then blew him away with her pragmatic reply. ''At any given point, at any given time, we're all desperate. That doesn't mean we're crazy. It means we're in need of an alternative. With alternatives come risks. I accepted that there was a risk in coming here. Just like you accepted a risk when you placed the ad.''

''A risk,'' he repeated, grunting, determined to ignore her logic. ''Playing the stock market is a risk. Running a red light is a risk. Your coming here goes way beyond risk. Your coming here—''

She cut him off. ''We made a bargain,'' she said with such soft entreaty that he had to stall the urge to ask her what the devil she was running away from.

''We both made a bargain,'' she repeated, as if that and that alone was the deciding factor.

While her emphatic, almost pleading conviction moved him, he pounced on her choice of words.

''You want to talk about bargains? Fine. I advertised for a bride—not a bride and a brat. Even if I had intended to follow through with this, you broke the rules when you brought your brother along.''

''About Mark...'' She hesitated, then gave a little shake of her head as the sound of his radio reached them from the loft at the far end of the cabin. ''I know. I know you didn't expect him. But he's really a good kid. He's just going through some bad times right now. He'll settle in. He won't be any problem.''

''You're missing the point,'' he enunciated in a tone that had made grown men break into a cold sweat.

Mackenzie Kincaid didn't have the sense to sweat or to cringe or to back down. She just sat there, a study in contrasts: stiff with determination, soft with vulnerability.

"I want to call this off," he said, angry with her for getting to him, angry with himself for letting her.

He waited for her reaction. When she just blinked, then lowered her gaze to the hands she'd wrapped tightly around her coffee cup, he swore under his breath.

"I'm sorry you came all this way." Even to his own ears it sounded like cold lip service. She made him feel like he'd just beaten a puppy. "I'm sorry. But there's not going to be a marriage."

He waited a beat, bracing for tears. He should have figured out by now that he wasn't going to get them. Not from her. She may look as fragile as a songbird, but she was as tough as nails.

He exhaled a deep breath and stayed the course. "Just as soon as this storm lifts and it's safe to make the trip, I'll drive you to Bordertown and put you and your brother on a bus back to L.A. I'll cover any costs you incurred getting here…and whatever else you feel you need for your trouble."

He expected any reaction but silence. He could have dealt with any reaction but silence.

With a frustrated growl, he slammed his mug on the counter. "Don't you get it? You're off the hook, green eyes. If you had any sense, you'd be breathing a big sigh of relief about now. I'm not going to make you go through with this farce."

She said nothing for a long moment. When she finally lifted her head, a new determination fired her eyes. She met his without flinching.

"Are you through?"

"Yeah," he snarled, her composure as irritating as a blister. "I'm through."

She rose from her perch on the chair, walked toward him in all her barefoot glory and met him toe-to-toe. "Then it's my turn to say *my* piece. Have a seat, Mr. Greene, while I spell a few things out for you.''

When she pointed a finger toward the table, he wondered if she realized she looked like David squaring off against Goliath. If so, it didn't faze her. She held her ground against him like a miniature marine. And as he trudged belligerently to the table, he had the unsettling thought that before she was through with him, he'd know exactly how Goliath felt.

Mackenzie wished she felt as confident as she sounded. She wished the beautiful and angry man facing her didn't scare the bejesuz out of her. And she hoped that her conviction to see this through packed enough punch to do the job. If he'd hit her with this last night, she'd have caved in, in a heartbeat. But she was rested now. And she was back in control.

She'd known this was coming. She also knew she would eat her pride—raw, well-done, stir-fried—any way he wanted to serve it to her, before she'd let him badger her into going back to L.A.

It was a cinch she couldn't outmuscle him. She needed a more powerful weapon than physical force. This morning she'd found it.

In this physically imposing, savagely strong specimen of a man, she'd discovered a major weakness.

The man had a need. A big one that encompassed both physical and emotional elements. His interaction with Mark was proof of the emotional need. He understood Mark. And in that little showdown before she'd taken her shower, he'd proven that he knew just how to handle him.

But the big surprise—and the weapon she suspected would ultimately win the war—was Abel Greene's physical need and the unbelievable but irrefutable fact that she'd tapped it.

As inconceivable as it seemed, brown-paper-wrapper-plain Mackenzie Jane Kincaid had gotten to him. She'd sensed it last night in the intense way he'd watched her. In the sullen way he stared into space when he thought she wasn't looking. She'd had lots of theories for what she'd sensed in him then, ranging from shock to impatience to heartburn.

Not until this morning in his office when he'd held her, and she'd felt the slight, but undeniable tremble of his big, strong body, had it occurred to her what was actually going on. She'd read the heat in his eyes, listened to the thunder of his heart as he'd fought for the control to back away—and she'd realized that he'd wanted to do more than just touch her. He'd wanted what men have wanted from women since the dawn of time. And he'd wanted it bad.

She'd tried to laugh herself out of that conclusion. It didn't seem possible. A man like him did not get in a foaming, fizzing lather about a woman like her. But as she'd stood in the shower, reliving the look on his face, the fire in his eyes, she'd accepted the heady truth. The man was hot for her body. Amazing. Simply amazing.

It wasn't that she was fooling herself into believing she'd suddenly turned into a siren. All she had to do was look in the mirror to be reminded of that. Hers was not the kind of face that launched ships—a dingy maybe—but never a luxury liner like Abel Greene. No. She knew that his physical response to her had more to do with—to use his word—*circumstances.*

He'd lived alone for a long time. Five years, if she remembered J. D. Hazzard's account accurately. Five years was a long time for a man as physical as Abel Greene to be without the comforts of the softer sex.

Mackenzie had never considered herself an opportunist—but she'd live and breathe the part if it meant keeping Mark alive. She may not be the game of choice, but she was the only choice and she was going to play Abel Greene's five years of solitude to her advantage. Sex was a powerful weapon. She'd never figured on owning the kind of firepower to employ it. Until this morning. And she'd been thinking about it ever since. Was it fair to Greene? No—but she was past the point of caring about fair play. And she wasn't going to think about what that made her. Too much was at stake. If she had to, she was going to brazenly dangle the golden sexual carrot in front of him until he broke from the pressure. And when she had him on his knees begging for release, she'd deliver the moon— just as soon as he married her.

Before she resorted to sexual warfare, though, she had some facts to lay out for him. A big, hefty guilt trip wasn't beyond her at this point. Even with her limited knowledge of his character, she was hopeful that he would buckle under the weight of it.

"You may feel you have a choice in this matter," she said, surprised that her voice came out so strong when her knees felt so weak. "But the truth is, *I* don't. When I answered your ad, I made a commitment. For me, there is no going back. I don't have anything to go back to. I quit my job. I sold everything I owned. Paid off every bill I had."

"Then I bought two one-way bus tickets, spent the last of my change in a crummy little truck stop for our breakfast yesterday morning, and as of right now I'm flat broke."

She paused to let him digest the facts.

"And why did I quit my job," she asked, when she was certain she had his full attention, "and deplete my funds? Because of you. Because *you* advertised for a bride. I answered that ad in good faith. And now I need you to fulfill your obligations."

She could have told him more. For now, though, she sensed that he didn't want to know the whole story. In the meantime, whether he knew or not didn't change anything. The issue was still the same. They couldn't go back.

Digging deep, she resorted to her big guns. Slowly, deliberately, she walked toward him and prayed the faraway sound of rap music meant Mark was still in the loft with his boom box. Heart pounding, her breath shallow, she stopped by his chair and with the sexiest look she could manage, gazed deep into his eyes. She didn't wait for his reaction. She didn't stop to ask herself, *Are you crazy?*

She attacked.

With calculated, and what she desperately hoped were seductive, movements, she eased onto his lap. He was so taken off guard, he didn't try to stop her. Instead his hands rose instinctively to her waist to steady her.

Running on the last of her resolve and a rush of breath-stealing adrenaline, she looped her wrists around his neck.

"Just so there's no question in your mind," she whispered, the uncertainty in her voice somehow coming out as a seductive rasp, "I want you to know that I intend to keep my part of the bargain. *Every* part of the bargain," she murmured, holding his dark, dangerous gaze as she leaned into him, pressing her breasts to his chest in a conscious attempt to increase his physical awareness of her as a woman.

She'd never vamped a man in her life. She didn't let that stop her from giving it her all now. Brushing her lips to his, slowly, provocatively, she played on one of the oldest laws of nature to drive her point home.

"I want to be your wife, Abel Greene." She nipped him lightly on his lower lip intending to seduce. But with a quickening of her heart and an unplanned lapse of purpose, she got caught up in the taste of him.

He tasted of danger. He tasted of need...and of a man standing on the edge of control. When his big body tensed in anticipation, she forgot she had a plan. She simply reacted. Tentatively she licked away the little sting her bite had given him.

"In every way...*every* way," she repeated, hearing a huskiness in her murmur that had eased in without conscious thought.

When she pressed deeper against his body, it was desire, not determination that prompted her. When he didn't pull away, it was temptation not calculation that had her slipping her fingers into the wealth of his thick, coarse hair, anticipation not manipulation that drew his mouth into more intimate contact with hers.

Temptress. Seductress. Wanton. They were new roles for her. But with Abel Greene's hard, hot body beneath hers, with his big hands stiffening in resistance, then clutching at her waist, she found herself melting to the task like butter over a flame.

His arms suddenly banded like steel around her. Against her breast she felt the thunder of his heart as he opened his mouth beneath hers and, with drugging urgency, stole the last conscious thought from her mind.

The plan had been to tempt him. The plan had been to tease with a kiss, suggest a promise. The plan had not included that he would respond with a passion so ravenous she thought he'd eat her alive with need.

She wasn't sure, but she guessed that she lost control about the same moment he did. Control didn't stand a chance as their bodies spoke, explored, tasted, then dissolved into a straining knot of feminine heat and masculine fire.

Without breaking the contact of their mouths, he lifted her, separated her thighs and resettled her so she was straddling his lap. Cupping her bottom with a possessiveness that stole her breath, he pulled her hard to his hips before tunneling up under her sweater, kneading, stroking, caressing.

She sucked in a harsh breath when his powerful, yet achingly gentle hand stole between their bodies, skated over her ribs and cupped a bare breast. Knotting her hands in his hair, leaned into the caress of his callused palm, all reason, all restraint eroded by the power and the explosiveness of his passion.

He groaned when she rocked against him. She sighed his name when he tore his mouth from hers and with teeth and tongue, laved the tender skin beneath her jaw.

When he roughly shoved her sweater up and out of his way, she arched toward him as he lowered his mouth to her breast.

"Help."

It could have been her calling out. Lord knows, she needed help. She'd planned on a kiss, not a quagmire of hot, mind-spinning caresses. She'd planned on a controlled, choreographed seduction, not a skidding, careening ride straight to the heart and the heat of an explosion.

It probably *should* have been her calling out, but it wasn't. The most she could possibly manage at the moment was a breathless, begging moan. And it couldn't have been Abel—his mouth was otherwise occupied. Wonderfully occupied, as he suckled and tugged and made sweet, savage love to her breast.

Through a haze of electric sensations, she heard the call again.

"Help…I think I need some help up here."

With a guttural curse, Abel tore his mouth away. Breathing hard, he cocked his head toward the sound.

Mark's tremulous plea reached them again from the far reaches of the loft, tentative with worry and concern.

"Hey…can anybody hear me? I think Nashata's having her puppies."

Frustration was a benign, inadequate description of how Mackenzie felt. Aggressive, blood-boiling need sizzled and seared through her veins, as she sagged against Abel's broad chest.

"I'll be right there." His voice rumbled against her ear, sounding strained, his breath serrated and irregular.

She was still trying to catch her own breath when his long, strong fingers tangled in her short hair. His grip tightened, then tugged her head back so he could look into her eyes. With his other hand he stroked his knuckles along her jaw, studying her face with eyes as hot as burning embers.

"You're playing with fire, little bird." He gave her hair a hard, but not hurtful, tug for emphasis. "If you come back to play again, make no mistake—you're going to get your feathers burned. And then we're both going to be sorry."

With a last dark look, he lifted her off his lap, set her down hard on the table and sprinted toward the loft.

"Oh, boy," Mackenzie breathed, lifting her hands to her cheeks and feeling the burn.

Nothing like that had ever happened to her before. Nothing even remotely like that had ever happened to her. She wasn't a virgin—but she'd strayed into virgin territory just now. At twenty-six, she'd had exactly two lovers in her life. One she'd intended to marry. When he'd skipped out for a thirty-six C-cup and an inheritance, she'd cried on a friend's shoulder. He'd been more than sympathetic. He'd taken her to his bed in a misguided attempt at loving away the pain.

In the end it had been a big mistake. But not nearly as huge as her little plan to seduce Abel Greene.

Neither one of her previous relationships had lit a fire like the one he'd just started. Sex with Steven had been safe, secure and totally predictable. Sex with Brian had been sweet and gentle. One brief, wild encounter with Abel Greene—hardly more than a kiss, really—had served notice on all of her erogenous zones that sex with this man would be unlike anything she'd ever experienced.

"Oh, boy," she murmured again. His morning stubble had left an erotically pleasant burn on the tender flesh of her breast. She touched her fingers to her mouth, still sensitized and gently throbbing from his kisses. And she felt the aching heat between her thighs that even now, after he'd dumped her on the table, grew in intensity.

"He's right about one thing," she mumbled, burying her face in her hands. "Fire has never burned this hot."

Gingerly she scooted off the table. With a trembling hand, she finger-combed her hair, made a valiant attempt at setting her clothes right and walked on shaky legs toward the loft.

Only a fool would follow him. But only a coward would avoid another confrontation. Besides, she needed an ally. Maybe she and Nashata could bond during the birth experience. And maybe she could use the time to figure out who had gotten the best of whom just now in Abel Greene's kitchen.

The birth process was new to Mackenzie. It was also everything it was cracked up to be. Frightening, enlightening, heartwarming. It was, in short, a miracle. It wasn't just the miracle of the new life of four wiggling, grunting puppies that brought tears to Mackenzie's eyes. It was the miracle of watching Mark let go of some of his street-smart, tough-guy machismo that he wore like barbwire around the sensitive and giving boy he'd once been.

She wasn't sure when or how it had happened, but somewhere between dusk and dawn, Mark and Nashata had found some common ground. And somewhere between adolescence and innocence, the sweet, impressionable little boy she'd watched grow into a troubled teen had turned a corner back toward the straight and narrow.

It was in the midst of this secondary miracle and Nasha-ta's spellbinding, three-hour ordeal, that the storm finally blew itself out. Mark, hovering like a fascinated midwife over Nashata and her brood, didn't notice the welcome intrusion of crisp, clear sunlight streaming through the peaks of the cathedral windows running the length of the loft.

Mackenzie noticed. She noticed the sudden absence of the tumultuous wind. She noticed the wary stillness of the man at her side. And she noticed the moment when the focus of his attention had shifted from Nashata and her pups to her face.

She felt the effect of his laser-sharp gaze in the places where he'd kissed her. She felt the struggle he was waging deep within himself—and the wanting that he ached to deny but couldn't.

But mostly she felt alive. Alive like she'd never felt in her life. She was aware of each breath she drew, of the rise and fall of her breasts beneath her sweater, of the fine, silky hairs at the nape of her neck, of the tenderness of her skin, the sensitivity of her nipples. And she knew he was aware of what his gaze was doing to her.

Slowly she closed her eyes. Slower still she opened them to look at the man who wanted so badly not to want her. Twin cylinders of glittering, golden light arrowed through the tall windows and poured over them like crystal rain as they knelt, side by side, near Nashata's makeshift whelping bed.

Abel was as beautiful by sunlight as he was by shadows and fire glow. His dark hair was highlighted to a blue-black sheen, his thick lashes tipped in feathery gold. But it was his face and the way the light played across the bronze planes of his cheeks and rugged jaw that defined and dramatized the character of the man within. And the inner struggle he was waging.

While she understood that he hadn't yet accepted their

fate, she felt enfolded in a warm, almost prophetic sense of rightness. In this unlikely place, at this unexpected time, she saw them kneeling together again—but at an altar, about to become husband and wife. And she wasn't afraid anymore.

She'd learned something about this man in the last three hours. All her uncertainty had left her as they'd held vigil over Nashata here in the loft. Abel Greene's gruff, stoic aloofness was a ruse. All the posturing about sending her away was a defense. The gentleness he'd shown with Nashata as she'd struggled to bring her puppies into the world, the patience he'd shown Mark, who had worried over the event like a nervous godparent, all spoke to qualities any woman would want in a man. It had also told her that he didn't really want to be alone. He had a lot to give to a relationship. He just didn't know it yet.

The fact that they barely knew each other was irrelevant. People married all the time and didn't *really* know each other. Her mother and father had been married almost twenty years. They still hadn't known each other when they'd parted ways.

Mackenzie wouldn't make that mistake. She might not know Abel now, but she would get to know this man. She wasn't foolish enough to believe in something as fanciful as love might actually happen between them. She'd come here accepting that and was willing to settle for mutual respect.

Coming to Abel Greene had been exactly the right thing to do. For both of them. In spite of his determination to do otherwise, she wasn't going to let him make the mistake of sending her back.

"It seems I need to thank you again."

They were sitting at the kitchen table some time later.

She'd followed him there after leaving Mark with Nashata and the pups.

He raised a fresh cup of coffee to his mouth.

She lifted her chin in the direction of the loft. "You were wonderful up there with Mark—the way you trusted him and made him feel you were counting on him to help you with Nashata."

He shrugged. "I did need his help."

"No, you didn't." Her smile was one of warmth and confidence. "Neither did Nashata. She was just doing what comes naturally. And I think you were doing what comes naturally, too. You made him feel necessary. Other than me, no one's ever extended that kind of trust to him before."

His response was to rise, snag his heavy coat from the coatrack by the door and shrug his broad shoulders into it.

"In case you hadn't noticed, the snow has stopped. As soon as I get the lane cleaned out, I'll take you back to the bus terminal."

Her heart fell. She'd known he wasn't ready to roll over and play dead in terms of allowing her to stay. But she had hoped she'd have some more time to convince him.

A quick glance out the window gave her new hope. There wasn't—in the most literal sense—a snowball's chance in hell that he was going to get that lane cleaned out anytime soon.

"It's going to take a mighty big shovel to clear out all that snow."

He shoved his hands deep into thick leather gloves. "It just happens I've *got* a mighty big shovel."

He snagged a set of keys from the key caddy by the door.

"You need keys for a shovel?"

"I need keys for the Cat."

She felt another stirring of unease. "Cat?"

"As in Caterpillar. I'll have the drive cleared out within the hour. You might want to use the time to pack."

"Well, hell," she sputtered, as she shivered in the wake of the winter-cold air that had sneaked in when he'd stalked out the door. "Now what are you going to do, Kincaid?"

As it turned out, she didn't have to do much of anything. Fate—and the interference of Abel's friends—did the doing for her.

Five

When she first heard the roar of an engine shortly after Abel stalked outside, she assumed he was firing up his plow. Then it dawned on her that the sound had started out faint and gotten louder.

Mackenzie scooted away from the table and peeked out the kitchen window—just as a pair of sleek, black snowmobiles crested a ridge and zigzagged through a stand of trees, shooting snow in their wakes.

She'd seen snowmobiles in pictures and films—but none had done justice to the gleaming pair of space-age-looking machines that slowed to a crawl, then idled to a stop by Abel's back door.

The riders were as futuristic in appearance as their transportation. Dressed in black boots and gloves, snug black suits and black, visored helmets, they looked like a pair of Darth Vader clones gone ice age. The drama of their entrance was offset only by the antics of a big, brown Labrador retriever that bailed out of the sidecar attached to the bigger machine.

Mackenzie watched as the riders each threw a leg over the back of their snowmobiles and stood, knee-deep in snow, while the dog leapt in comical, animated circles around them.

"Woa! Check out those machines."

"Yeah. Woa," she repeated, as Mark, apparently drawn by the roar of the engines, had left his vigil in the loft and joined her by the window.

"Who *is* that?"

As fascinated as Mark, she watched the pair approach the kitchen door. Even more fascinating was the way they met Abel there. The taller one of the two, obviously male and almost as tall as Abel, extended his hand. The smaller rider, undoubtedly female and model slim, embraced him.

"Looks like we're about to find out," she murmured, and braced herself for meeting some people who were evidently important to Abel.

"It's her," Mark whispered, just short of openmouthed gaping. He stared in star-struck awe as J.D. and Maggie Hazzard pulled off their helmets, zipped out of their snowmobile suits and made themselves at home in Abel's kitchen. "It's Maggie. *The* Maggie," he repeated, unable to stop himself.

The statuesque brunette, whose face and figure were recognizable to every male who had a heartbeat and every female who'd ever dreamed about being perfect, just smiled.

"She had that effect on me, too, the first time I saw her." A grinning J. D. Hazzard was quite openly as smitten as the rest of the world with his famous wife, who had recently, and at the top of her career, retired from the world of fashion modeling to try her hand behind the camera.

"But you get used to it after a while," he confided, and gave his wife a sympathetic look. "Too bad she's so plain. But hey, love is blind, right Stretch?"

"Deaf, too," Maggie retorted, with as much teasing warmth as her husband, "or I never would have fallen for that line of bull you dish out, Blue Hazzard."

Mackenzie listened to the playful banter, as overwhelmed as Mark by Maggie's beauty and fame. She was just as taken by J.D.'s blond good looks and how perfect the two of them looked together. Overriding everything, however, was the fact that the Hazzards had been the references listed in Abel's ad—and both of them had made it clear that they thought Abel Greene could walk on water and make it rain.

"Taking a bit of a risk—coming out in this snow, don't you think?"

This from a scowling Abel, who had been brooding and silent since he'd ushered the Hazzards into the cabin and made curt, unembellished introductions.

"No risk. Not now that the storm has blown itself out. You're forgetting, we're only ten minutes away by snowmobile. Besides, we were going a little stir crazy in the cabin."

"*Who* was going stir crazy?" The smile Maggie gave her husband sold him out.

"So when the sun came out to play," J.D. said, as if he hadn't heard her, "we came out to play, too."

"And to snoop," Maggie added with an apologetic glance at Mackenzie.

When J.D. winked at her, Mackenzie couldn't help but grin over his lack of guile.

"Okay, so we heard you had company over here. It was only the neighborly thing to do to extend a Northern Minnesota welcome."

"News travels fast," Abel grumbled, and they all knew that Scarlett had been busy on the radio.

J.D. ignored Abel's scowl, his grin encompassing the room in general before lighting on Mackenzie again. "It's nice to meet you in person, Mackenzie."

Clearly J. D. Hazzard wasn't going to be content until Abel's bare-bones introductions were fleshed out.

Abel's gaze cut to Mackenzie, the dark slash of his brows hooding his eyes. "In person?"

"I spoke with the Hazzards on the phone a couple of weeks ago."

"The ad, remember?" J.D. prompted. "When I sent it in, I listed Maggie and me as references."

Again Abel's gaze returned to hers.

"Well, it wasn't like I was going to come into this completely blind," she said defensively.

Maggie's soft, lyrical voice intervened, lessening the tight-wire of tension between them. "We're very excited about you being here, Mackenzie. But we're sorry you arrived in the midst of this terrible storm. Now that it's over, I'm sure Abel will show you how beautiful and how much fun Minnesota can be in the winter."

Mackenzie was tempted to tell them that the only part of Minnesota Abel wanted to show her was the part that appeared in a rearview mirror of a bus heading south.

She might have, too, if Nashata hadn't made an appearance right then.

"Nashata." Maggie reached out to pet the wolf dog. "How are you, girl?"

Hershey, the chocolate lab, who had until this time been lying on the rug by the door, rose with a tail-wagging, hip-wiggling gait and approached Nashata. The two animals nosed each other with affection.

"She had four puppies this morning," Mark volunteered, then turned a brilliant red when Maggie grabbed his hand.

"She had her puppies?" she squealed in delight.

"Hershey, you old dog you!" A grin split J.D.'s handsome face from ear to ear, his chest swelling like a proud grandfather's. "You're a daddy."

Mackenzie had to smile at the thought of the unlikely pair of animals together. The lab was as different from the wolf dog as silk was from sandpaper. As different as *she* was from Abel, she conceded on an afterthought, when their eyes met and held for a telling moment.

When Nashata nuzzled Hershey, then turned to leave the room and head for the loft, Hershey followed. If those two could get together, then there was hope for her and Abel. No matter how surly he looked at the moment.

"Can we see them?" Maggie asked, her excitement shining in her eyes. "Will it hurt anything if we take a peek?"

Mark looked to Abel for approval. When he nodded, Mark beamed.

"Come on. I'll show you where they are."

Abel wasn't sure exactly when he'd lost control over his life. He just knew that with Mackenzie Kincaid's appearance in it, control had slipped away like ice in a sun melt. With J.D. and Maggie's arrival he felt as if he'd become a spectator to a major disaster—a disaster he could do nothing to avert. It would have done no good to tell them that Mackenzie and her brother weren't staying. They wouldn't have listened, anyway. They were too busy interfering and matchmaking.

At Maggie's urging, Abel had reluctantly radioed Scarlett and Casey to tell them about the puppies. Even before he'd made the contact, he'd known the result. He'd promised Casey the pick of the litter. She'd been calling daily for the past two weeks, and he'd had no doubt she would badger her mother into coming over.

That's why, two hours later, he had a houseful of peo-

ple—all of them alternately cooing over the pups or grinning sly, expectant grins at him and Mackenzie. None of
them were the least bit successful in hiding the fact that
they thought the idea of him getting married ranked right
up there with winning the lottery.

Then there was the pot luck. Damned if they weren't
having pot luck in his kitchen. J.D. had run back home on
his machine and, following Maggie's instructions, had
brought half the contents of their refrigerator back to his
cabin. With the snow stopped and the snowmobile trails
clearly marked, it hadn't taken Scarlett and Casey long to
pack up their contributions and ride the trails from Crimson
Falls to his back door.

So here he was, sitting on the outer edge of four different
conversations—all of them less-than-artful attempts to find
out more about Mackenzie and Mark, and all of them, in
the process, dishing Mackenzie the goods on him.

He'd learned more than he'd wanted to about her. Like
the fact that she had worked as a bookkeeper for a small
paper supply company and had been going to school at
night studying business management. And that Mark liked
motors and music, in that order.

Of course, his friends made sure Mackenzie learned a
few things, too. J.D. was just putting the finishing touches
on the story about how the four of them—he, Maggie, J.D.
and Hershey—had put a dramatic end to a bear poaching
ring last summer, when Maggie gently but firmly called a
halt to the storytelling.

"Blue, stop. You're embarrassing Abel," Maggie ad-
monished J.D. "And you're embarrassing me."

"Because I called you an avenging angel?" J.D. grinned
unapologetically as Maggie reddened. "Well, hell, Stretch.
If you could have seen yourself, brandishing that shotgun
and telling that thug what for—"

"Enough," she insisted. "Eat. That ought to shut you up for a while."

But not for long, Abel realized, as he dug into his meal in silence and wondered how he was going to get out of this. Clearly everyone present—including a smiling Mackenzie Kincaid—assumed that they'd gone past the point of no return. Everyone had chalked this marriage up to a done deal.

As he sat there, listening to the good-natured joking and warm overtures of welcome toward Mackenzie and Mark, he actually found himself wishing it could happen.

He axed that thought in a heartbeat. What J.D. had with Maggie was special. It was also beyond him. He'd learned long ago that he wasn't like other people. Someone had always been willing to point that out to him. He'd made it a point to prove them right.

The Hazzards and Scarlett were among the few who accepted him as he was, no questions asked. He'd met Scarlett and Casey through J.D. and Maggie. An attractive strawberry blonde who'd passed her good looks on to her daughter, Scarlett was struggling to make a go of it with the historic Crimson Falls Hotel. It wasn't easy for a woman on her own. But then, life didn't often serve things up easy—as Scarlett knew too well.

She'd been stung by a bad man and a bad marriage. With pain came wisdom. She knew that happily ever afters were reserved for fairy tales and rare exceptions. Even at that, though, he could see in Scarlett's eyes that she envied the love Maggie and J.D. shared, even if she'd given up hope of having it for herself. And he could sense that she'd be as mad as a bear with its paw in a trap if she thought he was throwing away the chance to have it, too.

She didn't waste the opportunity to bring it up to him.

"I like your Mackenzie," she said softly, lagging behind

in the kitchen with Abel when the others had trooped into the living room by the fire.

"She's not *my* Mackenzie."

"Not yet," she said with gentle speculation. "But she can be. All you have to do is say the word."

He let out a deep, frustrated breath. "It's not going to happen."

"Oh, I know—it's not exactly conventional. But that doesn't mean it can't work. It's so…romantic," she added with a wistful smile, and tucked a runaway strand of hair back into her French braid.

He snorted. "It's lunacy and you know it."

She studied him closely. "No. I don't know it. And I think that even though you don't want to admit it, you want to go with this. I say, why not? Think hard—real hard, before you throw this chance away.

"Besides," she said, her eyes flitting to the living room where Mark and Casey had dropped their pretense of ignoring each other. "I think Casey's smitten. Mark, too. Those shy, flirty little glances they keep sneaking each other's way when they think no one's looking are sure signs of infatuation.

"Even though they got off to a rough start, I'd say that little girl of mine has a big bad crush on Mark. She'd never forgive you if you send them back to California before they even have a chance to have their first real fight. I overheard them making plans to meet tomorrow. Casey wants to come over and take Mark snowmobiling after she's had her fill of drooling over the puppies.

"Think about it real hard, my friend," she said in earnest, her gaze following his to where he had latched on to Mackenzie like a tractor beam.

With that, Scarlett walked out of the room, leaving him to either stew on that juice or join the gathering by the fire.

He opted for the shadows of the kitchen, even though

his gaze was drawn repeatedly to Mackenzie. The firelight glanced across her shining cap of flyaway hair. The smile on her face was open, accepting, attuned to the warmth extended around her.

He fought it, but as he watched her from this small distance, he was forced to admit that he liked seeing her here, in his home. He liked the way her eyes danced when she laughed. The way her breath caught on a sharp little hitch when she looked toward the kitchen and saw him staring.

And he liked—far too much—the fire that rolled through his blood when he thought of her slight, sexy little body pressed against his.

He clenched his jaw. The damn woman struck too many chords, played on too many weaknesses.

She wasn't the only one. Before he left, J. D. Hazzard played on a few of them, too.

"So," J.D. said, feeling his way carefully when he and Abel had left the women in the living room and Mark and Casey in the loft with the puppies. "Things are going well?"

Abel shut the door to his office behind them. "Things aren't going anywhere."

J.D. eased a hip onto Abel's drafting chair. "Right. And next you're going to tell me you don't find her attractive."

"Attraction has nothing to do with it."

J.D. quirked a brow and tucked his tongue in his cheek. "Stop gloating, Hazzard. I'm sending her back to L.A."

At that J.D. studied the can of soda dangling between his fingers. "Does she know that?"

"She knows. She just doesn't want to accept it."

"I guess I'm having a little trouble accepting it, too. What's the problem?"

Abel glared at him.

"Okay." J.D. held up a hand, conceding the point. "So

in theory, soliciting a bride isn't exactly a politically correct way to start a relationship. And in reality, if we hadn't been buzzed that night I never would have talked you into placing the ad.'' He grinned again. ''But hey, it's done. She's here. She seems like a nice woman. So why not at least give yourself a chance to get to know her?''

Abel walked to the window, wishing he hadn't been asking himself the same question ever since they'd sat in his kitchen and she'd laid into him about bargains and choices and risks—and then kissed him like she was trying to reinvent sin.

''You want to,'' J.D. stated, daring him to dispute it. ''It's obvious she wants to. Why fight it?''

''Even if I did want to, it couldn't go anywhere. I can't ask her to stay. Not now.''

J.D. cocked a brow. ''Not now? Not now, what?''

His friend knew him well. Well enough to wait until he decided to talk.

In the end Abel did just that. ''I've got a problem at the logging site,'' he said, turning back to face J.D.

His relaxed slouch was gone. His lazy grin had been replaced with an alert scowl. ''What kind of problem?''

There had been a time when he wouldn't have been able to place his trust in any man. Or woman. That had been before he'd met Maggie and J.D. It was a measure of how much stock he placed in their friendship that he confided in him now.

Methodically and concisely, Abel told him about the fire, about the problem with his machinery that had preceded it and about his suspicions that neither incident had been accidental.

''Who?'' J.D. simply said, not questioning why Abel suspected foul play.

His ready acceptance was another reason Abel valued J.D.'s friendship. He'd spent a lifetime justifying his existence and his motives. J.D. accepted his statement on blind faith.

"I can't prove anything. But I have my suspicions. Grunewald," he added, providing J.D. with the name of the owner of Grunewald-Casteele, the largest paper mill in the state.

"Why Grunewald?"

The question was not one of doubt but of curiosity.

"He wants my land."

J.D. snorted. "He owns three fourths of the timber in the state. Why would he want yours? You've got what—a couple hundred acres? Granted, it's choice, but it's like a grain of sand compared to Grunewald's beachful."

"It's not that he wants the land for the timber. It's more that he wants me off it."

"Why?"

Again, there was no doubt in his question, just more curiosity.

Unknowingly, Abel touched a hand to the scar that ran the length of his face. "We had a run-in once. Years ago. When I was a kid. A stupid kid," he amended, thinking back to a time when he'd strutted his pride like an invitation for someone to try to take it away from him. "He's still holding a grudge."

J.D. stared at Abel's scar and made the connection. "Grunewald did that to you?" Clearly shocked, J.D.'s eyes widened. "We always figured you'd had a run-in with a bear."

"No bear. Grunewald and a bunch of his buddies."

"He knifed you?" Disbelief colored each word.

Abel nodded. "Wanted to teach me a lesson. Put me in my place."

"Let me get this straight. He cuts you and you figure he's the one holding the grudge?"

"Oh, yeah. He's holding a grudge," Abel stated, picking up a glass paperweight from his desk and palming it.

"Why do I get the feeling there might have been a woman involved?"

A grim smile tipped up one corner of Abel's mouth. Absently he set aside the paperweight and resettled a hip against the edge of his desk. "I was eighteen. I was the 'breed' from the wrong side of the blanket. And I stepped across a line when I let a 'respectable' girl take her walk on the wild side with me."

"Let me guess. Grunewald considered her his property."

The smile, this time, was the smile of a cynic. "And now he considers her his wife."

J.D. let out a long, speculative breath. "That was a long time ago."

"It would have been...if she hadn't decided she wanted to pick up where she left off, when I came back to the lake."

Abel remembered clearly the night that Trisha Grunewald had shown up at his cabin looking for him. She'd had seduction on her mind and gin on her breath.

"I take it Grunewald found out."

Restless, Abel moved back to the window. "There was nothing to find out. Unless you count the fact that I turned her down flat."

"Then why..." Realization dawned before J.D. finished his question. "Never mind. I think I got it. A woman scorned and all that."

He shrugged. "That's my guess. She was pretty hot. She left here spitting like a cat and promising she'd make me pay. It was a couple of years ago, but I figure she's been working on Grunewald ever since, and he's finally decided that since he couldn't buy me out, he'd force me out."

"So he's tried to buy you out?"

"Several times. Just like he's already bought out everyone else." He paused as J.D. stared in thoughtful silence, then downed the last of his soda in one swallow.

"This was all Chippewa land at one time," Abel went on, sharing with J.D. what others had only speculated about. "When a Frenchman from Quebec married my great-great-grandmother, he bought this tract of timber for her as a wedding gift so she would never have to leave her home. When she passed it down, it was with the stipulation that it would never be sold out of the family. My mother honored her wishes." What he couldn't bring himself to confide—what he'd never confided to anyone—was that her determination to pass the land on to Abel had probably cost her her life.

"Grunewald will never get this land."

If J.D. was aware of the anger that twisted in Abel's gut, he wisely let it alone.

"So what do you want to do about it?" he asked instead.

Abel shook off the memories. "Nothing. Not yet. So far nothing has been damaged too badly. I'll wait him out a little longer. Either he'll tire of his little game or he'll tip his hand. Then I'll confront him."

"We'll confront him," J.D. amended. "I've got no time for a back-stabbing s.o.b."

"It could get ugly."

"It's already ugly," J.D. said, prepared to back him all the way.

Abel didn't verbalize his appreciation. He knew he didn't have to. Instead, he reinforced his argument about Mackenzie. "And that's why she can't stay. Even if I wanted her to, I don't want her or the kid getting into the middle, if it blows up."

J.D. considered him for a long moment. "I'm not going to pretend that if Grunewald is behind this that he'll stop short of violence. I've heard stories of his extreme methods of making deals to get what he wants. But I think you're selling Mackenzie short. A woman who would give up everything she knows to marry a man sight unseen strikes me as someone who can hold her own. Besides, Grunewald's quarrel is with you, not her.''

It was the same argument he'd been having with himself every time he'd come close to reconsidering his decision to send her away.

"And I know you," J.D. continued. "You won't let Grunewald get near her or her brother."

That much was true. He protected what was his.

That thought stopped him cold. Mackenzie Kincaid wasn't his to protect. No matter how badly everyone else seemed to want her to be.

A soft rap on the door sent both their heads around.

Maggie poked her head inside. "When did this turn into a private party?''

J.D. grinned and tucked her under his arm when she walked into the room. "Men stuff. You wouldn't understand.''

"Stow it, Hazzard," she said with a smile warm enough to melt ice. "Why don't you scoot? It's my turn to have a shot at him.''

"You're in trouble now, Greene," J.D. warned. After planting a kiss on his wife's brow. "And you're on your own with this one." He stopped, one hand cupping the open door. "Just remember what I said." Then he planted a kiss on Maggie's cheek.

"The man's insufferable," she said on a sigh, as J.D. shut the door behind him.

Abel studied her face and saw what he wanted to see. "And you love him for it.''

"Yes. I love him. For that and for much, much more.''

She hesitated then, just long enough for Abel to sense what was coming.

"Is this going to be another lecture on how I can have that, too, if I just give it a chance?"

She smiled. "We've been working you over pretty good, huh?"

He grunted.

"It's because we care about you. And after today, it's because we care about Mackenzie and Mark."

He turned his back to her, fighting to maintain his resolve.

"I'm not going to push, Abel. I'm just going to ask you to think about the possibilities. I never thought I'd find what I have with Blue. Now I can't imagine life without him."

She walked up behind him, placed a hand on his shoulder. "Don't do something you'll regret."

Then she left him alone.

"All in all, Mackenzie Kincaid," she told herself brightly, "it's been quite a day."

Hah! That was like saying the Concord was just a plane. "Or that Abel Greene is just a man," she murmured, looking out the kitchen window, watching for his snowmobile with him and Mark on board to come back home.

Home. She closed her eyes and backed away from the window. She'd have to be careful about that. She'd been here less than twenty-four hours—an eventful twenty-four hours, granted—and she was already thinking of this cabin as home.

"You've got a ways to go before you'll be solid on that count," she reminded herself, as she slipped through the living room and climbed the loft steps to check on Nashata and the pups.

"How's it going, girl?" she whispered, as the new mother nuzzled her babes protectively, then laid her head back down in a gesture of trust.

The sun was low on the horizon now. Almost two hours

had passed since the Hazzards had loaded up Hershey and headed for their cabin, which she now knew was just a few miles up the shoreline of the lake. Almost two hours since Abel, with Mark on board—pretending he wasn't excited—left on Abel's big, black machine to accompany Scarlett and Casey back to the hotel nestled deep in the north woods.

"We're going to ride with them back to the hotel," Abel had said, then paused and added gruffly, "so I don't have to worry about them running into trouble." Then he and Mark had headed out the door.

"I figure he went with them so he could get away from me for a while. What do you think, Nashata?"

Nashata. She'd heard Abel tell Mark it meant little chief. He'd named her that because he'd found her beside the body of her mother who'd been killed by a poacher's bullet. As hungry and as frightened as she'd been, she'd still scrapped and snarled when Abel had picked her up and brought her home.

"Like a little chief," he'd said.

"He's taken good care of you, huh, girl?" She stroked Nashata's coarse gray coat. "Think we can convince him he can take good care of me, too?"

The thought came unbidden. She'd always taken care of herself, always stood on her own two feet. But, oh, just once, it would be nice to know that if she stumbled, if she had a need, that someone like Abel would be there to lighten the load.

She stopped that train of thought abruptly. Self-pity was a luxury she couldn't afford. It was a place she didn't let herself go very often. And she had no time for crybabies.

It was almost dark when she slipped down the stairs to make some hot chocolate. She'd just set it off the burner when she heard the roar of the snowmobile.

Mark burst into the cabin in a flurry of crisp, winter-cold air and red cheeks.

"Man, oh, man. Talk about a trip. That snowmobile is one bitchin' machine! The sucker flat-out flies."

"And hello to you, too." She grinned as she reached for mugs from the cupboard.

"Yeah, hi," he said quickly, and then went on, unaware that he was prattling with excitement as he shrugged out of his coat and the cap and gloves Abel had loaned him for the trip.

"You ought to see that old hotel where Casey and her mom live. It's like, way cool. It must be a hundred years old. The floors are all wavy and there are all these neat old pictures everywhere. It even has a ghost. Honest to God," he added when she shot him a skeptical frown. "I'm going to go check on Nashata."

And just that fast he jogged out of the kitchen and raced up the stairs.

He didn't see the tears crowding her eyes. Didn't know that in the past twenty-four hours she'd seen more glimpses of the little boy she loved than she had in the past two years. Couldn't possibly be aware that her happiness over this rebirth of innocence had brought tears that just would not remain unshed.

And Abel, when he found her like that in the kitchen a few minutes later, couldn't possibly know that she felt she owed him much more than her thanks for giving her back her brother.

Six

Abel didn't want to know what had prompted her tears, though he figured it had to do with Mark. He didn't want to know any more about her, either, though he suspected there was a lot more to learn.

What he wanted was to untie this unfamiliar knot of awareness in his gut when he looked at her—and put to rest the ridiculous notion that there could possibly be a future for him with Mackenzie Kincaid.

What he wanted was to get them gone before he got in any deeper.

He'd have accomplished it, too, if it hadn't been for the impromptu gathering his friends had arranged that afternoon. It was too late to plow the drive now. That meant he was stuck with her for another night. It didn't mean he had to like it.

The unsavory truth, however, was that if he let himself, he could like it. He could like it far too much. Just as the possibilities his friends had encouraged him to think about appealed too much.

She settled across from him by the fire and handed him a mug of hot chocolate.

"Maggie tells me you built the cabin."

He responded with silence.

"She said that's what you do. For a living, I mean. You build houses."

"I build log cabins," Abel clarified. He heard the gruffness in his voice and felt compelled to soften his tone when he continued. "And yes, it's a source of income."

But not his only source.

A greater source was the interest he drew from bounties he'd collected during his years as a mercenary fighting the dark world of drug trafficking.

He wondered what little Mackenzie Kincaid would think if she knew about the ugliness of his past. For a moment he even considered telling her enough to scare her off. In the next moment he reconsidered, afraid it would do just that.

He damned himself for a fool. *Indecision* was not a word in his vocabulary. Neither was *waffling*. Yet he'd been doing plenty of both ever since he'd found this pretty little bird in the snow.

"You don't have a lot to say, do you?"

Her soft query brought his head up. There was no bite in her words. Frustration added teeth to his response. "Seems to me that with you around, I don't have much need."

She smiled, a soft, good-natured concession, ignoring his barb. "You're not the first person to imply that sometimes I talk too much."

Not for the first time her smile caught him off guard.

Not for the first time he did something foolish because

of it. "As long as you're talking, why don't you level with me?"

He had no idea why he'd opened up that door. Didn't like much the thought of hearing something he might not want to deal with. But the words were out, and suddenly he needed to know. "Why did you come here? I don't understand. You're a young, attractive woman. You didn't have to resort to a personal ad to get a man. So why? Why did you leave everything that's familiar for nothing but unknowns?"

Caution darkened her eyes—as if she were weighing the consequences of confiding in him. He called her on it. "Don't wimp out on me. now, green eyes. And don't give me any bull about being a free, California spirit following your karma or any other crap. Level with me. You're here because you're running from something, aren't you?" The look on her face told him he'd nailed it. "I have a right to know what it is."

She looked away. Looking guilty. Then looking determined.

"You're right. You do have a right to know."

She drew in a bracing breath, sent him a considering look and without preamble started talking. "My parents aren't exactly parent-of-the-year material," she began, looking away to watch the inane activity of her hands as she ran her thumb along the lip of the mug.

"I was the reason they got married," she said. "Mark was the reason they stayed together. In between they either fought like dogs over a bone or treated each other to long, empty silences."

A pensive moment followed, and he suspected she was reliving some of those scenes in her mind.

"I handled it better than Mark," she finally said. "I don't know why. And I don't know why they stayed together as long as they did."

He didn't prompt. He just sat, neither looking at her or away. Just listening and knowing that in the process, damn her, she was going to make him care a little more about her and her brother.

"I'd already moved out by the time they split up five years ago. I was twenty-one and making it...barely," she amended with a tight, grim smile, "on my own. Mark was only ten. The divorce hit him hard. He was still young enough to believe that things weren't as bad as they seemed...and that maybe if he was good enough, it would get better."

She smiled again, sadly this time. "It's awful, isn't it, what little kids take on when the adults in their lives let them down?" She shook her head, looking into space. "Oh, I know. What happened to Mark isn't anything new, nothing that hasn't happened to thousands of other kids when their parents divorce. But there was just one little twist that made it tougher for him to take.

"Most parents fight over who gets custody. Not mine." Again, a bitter smile. "With their divorce came liberation. They decided it was time to dip their toes in that wild singles pool they'd left behind. Neither one of them wanted Mark around slowing them down."

She let her anger really show then. In the clipped edge to her voice. In the grim set of her mouth. "No kid deserves what they did to him. It was bad enough that they didn't want him around. But they had to let him know it. Two years ago, when I realized how badly it was affecting him, I brought him to live with me. Except, I'd waited too long."

Only his silence prompted her to continue.

"He fell in with the worst crowd possible. He started getting into trouble with the law. Minor scrapes at first, but still dangerous, considering what he might soon do—or what he might already be doing but just wasn't getting caught at.''

Again her gaze dropped to her mug. Again she ran her thumb along the rim of it, regret showing in the droop of her small shoulders. "I should have taken him with me sooner. I should have gotten him out of that situation where Mom and Dad passed him back and forth, each change of custody destroying more of his self-esteem. Maybe he wouldn't have gotten so far off track.''

Exhaling deeply, she let her head fall back against the sofa and stared at the ceiling. He could almost feel the guilt and regret she had taken on, pressing down on her like lead. When her eyes—old, wise, weary—sought his again, he didn't look away.

"One night he came home wearing gang colors. I knew then that I'd lost him. The gangs and the guns and the gutter had sucked him in. And when, soon after that, he came home bloody and beaten and crowing that he'd come of age because a rival gang had made a death threat against him, I knew I had to get him out of there. He was marked in L.A. And it was just a matter of time before they killed him.

"That's when I ran across your ad,'' she said, holding his gaze levelly. "I was on break at work and someone was giggling over the extreme measures a person would take just to get a little—'' she cut herself off with a delicate smile "—company.''

Growing increasingly more uncomfortable, with both her candor and the magnetic pull of her eyes, he rose and added more wood to the fire.

"I laughed, too,'' she said, as he stabbed at the flames with the iron poker. "At first. But I hadn't come up with a solution to Mark's problem. Every day I lived in fear that he wouldn't live to see the next one. I had to get him out of L.A., but we couldn't just relocate. That took money. Money I didn't have.

"My parents weren't an option. I couldn't send him there. After all they'd done to him, he would have just run away. And I'd promised myself and Mark that I'd always be there for him."

He heard her shifting and settling deeper into his sofa, but he didn't turn around.

"I kept thinking about your ad. A part of me was appalled by the idea of answering it. But when nothing else presented itself, I began looking at it more and more as a viable option. You offered security. Safety. Seclusion.

"And then something happened that made the decision for me."

The desolation in her voice had him turning to face her.

"A boy was shot. A fourteen-year-old kid. In front of our apartment building. A boy who looked like Mark—by a bullet that was meant for him. I answered your ad the next day."

She closed her eyes, shook her head. Swallowed hard. Then met his gaze.

"Was I scared? Yeah. I was scared. The thought of actually committing to this outrageous agreement scared the bejesuz out of me. The reality was, I was willing to make a life commitment to a stranger. The *harsh* reality was, if I didn't, I was going to lose my brother. Either way, I was damn scared."

He couldn't look away from her.

"Ask me if I'm afraid now, Abel."

Her voice held him with the same strength as her gaze.

"Ask me," she repeated softly, "if after seeing you with my brother, after seeing you bring out a spark of the little boy behind those hoodlum eyes, after seeing him safe, if my desperation paid off."

He braced a palm on the mantel and made himself look away.

"I'm not afraid anymore," she said on a whisper. "I'm not feeling desperate anymore. I'm confident that there is a place here for Mark. That there's a place here for me.

"You've given me an option, Abel. The only one I have. And if you'll give me the chance, I'll put everything I have into making it work."

The conviction in her voice made his chest hurt.

He needed to say something. He needed to warn her that she'd be running from one source of heartache to another if she hitched her hope to the likes of him.

But he didn't. He couldn't. In truth, he didn't want to. He wanted to think about what she'd told him. He wanted to accept the trust she'd invested in him.

And underlying it all, he wanted to savor the sound of her voice saying his name. Like satin and softness it wove itself around him. Like sin and salvation it tempted him to let her stay.

The cabin suddenly seemed cramped and suffocating. As big as it was, there wasn't enough room to contain all the feelings that closed in on him.

Without a word he walked away. Snagging his coat, he shrugged into it and stalked outside. He fed the horses. Stayed with them for a very long time. Thinking of her honesty. Humbled by her valor. Damning her candor—and damning his desire to do right by her.

He felt cornered. Backed against the wall. She was asking too much. She was asking if she could put her trust in him. A trust he hadn't earned. A trust he'd told himself was only for hire when there was money on the line.

He almost wished she'd tried to lie to him—told him some whopping sob story about why she needed him to let her stay. Then he'd have had just cause and no problem to claim "no sale." But he'd dealt with deception the better part of his life, and he knew the truth when he heard it.

She hadn't asked for herself. She'd asked for the boy's sake. His motives for placing the ad paled in comparison to hers. His excuse had been too much whiskey and self-pity. Hers had been a matter of life and death.

He didn't doubt for a second that the boy was in danger in L.A. He'd seen enough of the streets in the years he'd worked undercover to know Mark was as good as dead if a gang had targeted him.

This was no longer about what he needed. It was about life and death. Yet as he'd listened to Mackenzie and realized the seriousness of her situation, one selfish, forbidden thought kept hammering at him: *Here's your chance. Here's your chance to have something good.*

When he let himself in through the kitchen door an hour later, two voices raised in laughter rang down from the loft, one soft and feminine, the other young, but distinctly masculine.

They were sounds that had been missing too long from this house—this house that he'd built big enough for a family, but had filled with nothing but silence.

He looked around the kitchen, into the living area, thought of his big, empty bed, of a woman's warmth. For the first time since all this started, he imagined himself coming home to these sounds each day. Imagined the nights filled with something other than empty darkness.

Imagined, finally, with his heart pumping, the devastation Mackenzie could cause if he let her become a part of his life and then someday she decided to walk away.

Sleepy-eyed, her hair tousled, her cheek still creased from a restless night on the sofa, Mackenzie gazed at Abel's sullen face over her morning coffee.

True to form he glared back.

His hostile look shouldn't have elicited a shudder of arousal in her. But arouse her, he did. And a shudder was the least of what she felt when she looked at him.

He made her fantasize of feather beds and vibrant sunsets. Roaring fires and heated skin. Husky moans and sizzling passion.

And he made her want to believe again, in the hopes and dreams she'd given up long ago as lost.

Feeling herself redden, she turned away.

Guilt nipped at her. This wasn't about her. This was about Mark and what he needed.

Abel knew all there was to know now. She'd told him the whole story last night. She only wished she knew what he was going to do about it.

Last night he'd slipped quietly back into the cabin while she was still up in the loft. The door to his bedroom was closed when she'd come downstairs.

She'd thought of going to him there. To ask if he'd changed his mind. To risk the last of her pride if he hadn't.

When she'd realized she was motivated by her own needs as much as by Mark's, she couldn't do it. Instead she'd lain awake half the night wondering why a man who looked like him, who engendered the trust and friendship of people the quality of the Hazzards and Scarlett Morgan, needed to solicit a wife. And she wondered what he'd decided to do about the one he had for the taking.

He had his secrets, too, she was sure of it. He had his own set of sorrows and sins to deal with. It was unnerving that this intriguing paradox of fire and ice, strength and vulnerability could foster protective needs in her. And wanting.

Even more unsettling was the knowledge that he held their future in his hands.

It was an awesome concept. A monster disadvantage.

And even though she knew she could still say the word and the deal would be off, she wasn't even tempted to say it. Not now. Not now that she'd met him, not now that she'd kissed him and he'd made her feel alive like she'd never felt in her life.

She was so engrossed in those feelings that it took her a moment to realize he'd just said something critical.

She sat up straight in her chair. "I'm sorry. What did you say?"

"I said the winters here are hard and long."

Her eyes arrowed to his, searching and alert, as she studied his savagely beautiful face. What she saw there reinforced the significance of his statement.

With reluctance he was telling her she could stay—and in the same breath warning her away.

Her heart thrummed with anticipation and relief.

"Your fire is warm and inviting," she said softly, telling him she understood and was up to the challenge.

It didn't appear to make him happy. "The springs and summers are too short."

She worked to hide a small, triumphant smile. "I've had enough year-round California summers to last a lifetime."

"I'll be gone sometimes," he countered, holding her unwavering gaze. "My work requires it. Not just at the logging site. I'll have to go out of state occasionally—for materials, to tie up contracts."

Give it your best shot, Abel Greene, she challenged silently, basking in the light of her victory. *You're not going to scare me off.* "A man has to work, or he's not a man."

He took a deep swallow of coffee. Stared at his hands. "It could be hard on you…this place. The isolation. Being alone."

There was so much knowledge of the word *alone* in his voice, *she* felt the pain she knew he'd never admit to. She could only guess at the loneliness he must have felt in the course of his life. Her smile turned bittersweet as his gaze shifted toward the window.

"I've been alone most of my life, too," she said softly. "I expect this to be an improvement."

She felt something then that she suspected he'd deny to the nth degree. A bond. They were worlds apart, yet in that moment she knew something of where he'd come from and likened it to where she'd been.

"You'll get bored," he said abruptly.

She couldn't help it. She laughed when he stubbornly refused to give it up.

"Hardly."

He drew another contemplative breath, frowned at his cup. "Mark will have to go to school."

"Amen to that."

"His problems are far from over. He's still an angry, mixed-up kid."

"But he's on his way to healing. I have you and this place to thank for that."

"Don't," he said so sharply she flinched. "Don't put your stock there. I'm no role model. And I don't want to be."

"I think it's too late," she said carefully, puzzled by the sudden harshness of his words. "He wouldn't admit it, but Mark already looks up to you."

He slowly shook his head, a tight, cynic's smile lifting one corner of his mouth. "You're really good, green eyes."

The ice in his tone chilled her.

"You did a real number on me last night. Pushed all the right buttons. But you've already got what you wanted...so don't push any harder, okay?"

His eyes had grown hard, his mouth grim. "I accept the responsibility for your coming here. I understand that you can't go back. For that reason, I won't send you away. But don't read more into my decision than is there. Starting with your skewed perception of my effect on your brother—'' She hadn't yet recovered from that blow, when he hit her hard and low with another. ''—and ending with any notion you might have that there will ever be anything between us but a physical and a business relationship.''

Because he carried his own scars, Abel knew that not all wounds bleed. The devastation on her face was proof that he'd cut deep. She'd lost all color, all light from her eyes. He regretted causing her pain, but better now than later. He was guilty of a number of sins, but feeding her illusions wouldn't be one of them.

He could not let himself get close to this woman. He couldn't afford to. Wasn't sure he could survive it.

Last night she'd brought him close—so close—to exposing the weakness he'd guarded the better part of his life: the wanting to let someone in.

He'd imagined himself opening that door to her—only to have her slam it in his face. Just thinking of the damage she could do had been enough to set his head back on straight. And now she knew where she stood.

Though it went against his better judgment, he would let her stay. His conscience wouldn't allow him to let her leave, now that he knew her story. While he felt a legitimate concern that Grunewald might be a threat, L.A. was a bigger threat to her and Mark. And J.D. was right. Grunewald's quarrel was with him, and if it did extend to Mackenzie and Mark, he'd make damn sure nothing happened to them.

"This is your last chance to back out," he said. "If you stay, it will be as my wife. I'll see to your needs and I'll expect you to see to mine. But that's as far as it goes. Are we clear?"

He endured the silent probe of her eyes. He knew she was looking for a sign...any sign that there was something more than cold, calculated reserve behind his blunt ultimatum.

"As crystal," she finally said. "As my husband you'll take care of me. As your wife I'm expected to take care of you...in bed."

The defeat in her voice almost blew his defenses out of the water. He closed his eyes. Swallowed hard. Wanted, in that moment, to be more than he was, more of what she needed him to be. But it wasn't that simple. Just like life wasn't simple or sympathetic or even sane.

That was the crux of this entire miserable mess. There was nothing sane about wishing he could give her all the things a woman like her deserved. There was nothing sane about the way she'd reduced him to wanting.

And he did want her. He'd wanted her from the moment she'd vaulted onto his back, clawing and pecking at him like a mother bird protecting her young.

"It won't be unpleasant for you." That much he could give her. "But if you expect more, you'll only be disappointed."

She looked out the window. Gave a small resigned shake of her head. "I learned about unrealistic expectations a long time ago."

When she faced him again, he saw that the fire was back in her eyes. So was the grit that had gotten her this far. But the soft light of hope was gone...and for that he was sorry.

He offered the only explanation he could. "It's all I have to give. I'm sorry."

Her chin raised a notch. "No need. And don't worry. I made a bargain. I'll stick to it."

"It's the wilderness, for pity's sake," J.D. groused, his voice rusty with sleep when Abel raised him on the radio a few minutes later. "You'd think a man could sleep in, in his own cabin, in his own bed, without the neighbors waking him up."

"Call the preacher."

Silence. Then "Huh?"

"Call him and find out when we can do the deed."

Abel's hands were sweating when he flipped off the switch.

It was done. Or it soon would be.

Bundled up in boots, a warm coat and the scarf and gloves she'd bought in town yesterday, Mackenzie slipped out of the cabin while J.D. and Abel and Mark and Casey moved Nashata and the puppies from the loft to the empty spare bedroom and Maggie and Scarlett fussed with details and decorations.

It was December the nineteenth.

Her wedding day.

She needed some time to herself before the ceremony, slated for three o'clock that afternoon.

It was early yet, a little after one, plenty of time to enjoy a few moments of this sparkling, beautiful day.

The sun was blade bright. The air was so crisp and clean it made her lungs burn. Evergreens, draped in their very best snow-laced gowns, crowded around the cabin in the woods like hovering guests, waiting for a glimpse of the bride and groom.

If she could chance believing in omens, this bright, sunny day would bode well for her future as Abel Greene's wife...and the devil with what he'd said.

Buoyed by renewed hope and an optimist's determination, she listened to the sound of the snow crunching under her feet, the call of a blue jay as it flitted from tree to snow-laden tree—to the inherent peace and pure, uninhabited silence of this winter wonderland.

This would be her home now. This would be the place

where Mark would grow to manhood and where, quite possibly, she would raise children of her own.

A soft smile lifted her lips as she burrowed her chin deeper into the fur-lined collar of her coat. She liked the idea of children. As improbable as it seemed, she liked it a lot.

What also seemed impossible was that she was about to marry a man she'd known for a sum total of five days. Not only was she looking forward to sharing his bed, she was looking forward to sharing his life—even though he'd gone out of his way to point out that there would be no love in their relationship. Sex, yes. But never love.

She hadn't come here expecting that, so his cold, harsh assessment of their life together shouldn't have hurt her. But it had.

As she'd sat there two mornings ago, stunned by his bluntness, she'd realized she'd been lying to herself. In spite of all her posturing about being prepared to accept whatever he gave her, the reality was she wanted more. She'd always wanted more. Abel's bluntness had sliced like a knife.

So at first she'd hurt for herself. She'd mourned what was not to be. Wallowed in missed opportunities and the loss of her romantic hopes. It wasn't that she thought she loved him. It was that she wanted to and she'd hoped that he might want to care about her, too.

That morning in his kitchen he'd slammed the door on either possibility.

When she'd gotten past the disappointment, it had come to her that something wasn't quite right with the picture he'd painted. He'd worked a little too hard to convince her he was uncaring, unfeeling and indifferent. She hadn't been able to see it at first—she'd been too busy nursing her own wounds to realize that he was wounded, too. And he was protecting himself by shutting her out.

At length the true picture had fallen into place, and she'd realized what she was really up against. She'd finally understood why a man like him would resort to advertising for a bride, then lay out the ground rules like clauses in a contract.

It wasn't that he was indifferent. It wasn't that he was cold and calculating. A man without feelings wouldn't have gone to such extremes to warn her away.

What Abel Greene was, she'd concluded after reading all the signs, was afraid. Afraid of commitment. Not because he couldn't accept the responsibility. But because commitment required a large degree of trust. Trust required opening himself up to the possibility of getting hurt. And everything about this man—from his hard, hungry eyes, to his staunch, schooled denial—suggested he'd endured all the hurt he could handle in his life.

He was, by intent, a recluse. He was a man who entrusted his friendship to a select few. A lonesome man who had not yet accepted that it was all right for him to not want to be alone.

His interaction with Mark supported that conclusion. He understood Mark. She'd watched them together these last two days. The bond between them had grown as they cared for Nashata and the pups, chopped wood, took care of the horses or talked quietly of the lake and this land—the one thing Abel didn't pretend to be indifferent to—and she was delighted to see Mark's anger erode inch by inch.

Abel Greene could claim he didn't care until the snow melted. For his sake she wasn't going to buy it. His sake and hers and Mark's. If for no other reason than that he was giving her brother back to her, she was going to make him see the light.

She brushed away a tear with her gloved finger. "You're a melancholy sap, Kincaid," she sputtered with a sniff, and refocused her thoughts. "And today you'll become a wife."

Bless J.D. and Maggie and Scarlett. As soon as Abel had given the nod, they'd sprinted into action, determined to make this a special, memorable occasion.

As Abel had complacently let them prepare the cabin for the ceremony, she'd gotten an even stronger sense that he wasn't dreading it as much as he let on.

"At least the part that involves the marriage bed," she whispered aloud, drawing in a deep breath of cold, bracing air.

She'd made some big promises that first morning in his kitchen. Promises that went far beyond what her limited sexual experience could fulfill. What if she disappointed him?

What if he disappointed her?

A nervous laugh burst out with thought, ringing softly through the forest. As if a man like that could possibly disappoint any woman.

"I can't believe you can find anything to laugh about."

She whipped around at the sound, her laughter drifting away at the defensive set of Mark's shoulders and the darkness of his brooding scowl.

While he had come a long way she'd sensed his seesawing emotions during the wedding preparations of the past two days. She had been tempted to ask. But she'd also learned something about patience in dealing with her brother. Mark had come out here for a reason. If he wanted to talk about it, it was up to him to initiate the dialogue.

So she waited, instead of prodding him.

Finally, after looking at everything but her, he let it out. "You're marrying him because of me."

She stuffed her gloved hands deep into her pockets. "I've made worse bargains in my life."

Tears filled his eyes. Tears he quickly blinked away with

an angry jerk of his chin and enough determination to will the wind to stop. "You shouldn't have to. You shouldn't have to bargain because of me."

"If not for you," she said quietly, "then who should I bargain for?"

He hunched his shoulders and showed her his back.

"I love you Mark," she added after a stretch of silence. "But I'd lost you and I wanted you back."

Head down, he plodded to a jack pine and picked absently at the bark.

"I like it here." His voice was choked with more guilt at the admission. "I don't want to go back to L.A. If I was a man, I'd lie and tell you I did. I'd convince you I wanted to go back so you could go back to your life. And then you wouldn't have to marry him."

Her own eyes filled with tears as she walked up close beside him. "I thought you liked Abel."

He sniffed and batted at the tree trunk with a booted foot. "I do. But you're the one who has to marry him."

She reached for him then, cupped his slim shoulders in her gloved palms and turned him to face her. "He's a good man, Mark. I could do worse. Much worse. And here's something else you need to know. I like him. I like him a lot.

"This is going to be good," she assured him, responding to the turmoil in his eyes. "For all three of us."

His look held so much guarded hope she threw caution to the wind and tugged him into her arms. The old Mark would have backed angrily away. The new one let her hold him.

"I know you'll find this hard to believe, but I think maybe Abel needs us as much as we need him."

Her statement brought a snort from him and the last of his patience with her sisterly embrace. He pried himself out of her arms. "Abel doesn't need anybody."

The simple, straightforward words spoke of hero worship. She understood that. She also understood that Mark had just voiced her biggest fear where Abel Greene was concerned.

For the first time since coming outside, she felt a deep, worrisome chill. She prayed that Mark was wrong. She prayed that in the days, the weeks, the years to come, that the man she was going to marry would come to care about and need her as much as she did him.

"Come on," Mackenzie said, pushing her concerns aside and heading for the cabin. "Let's go see if everything's ready up there."

Including the bridegroom, she thought, pushing aside the fear that he might leave her standing at the altar.

Seven

They'd turned the cabin into a cathedral. Maggie and Scarlett insisted that with its lofty ceilings and towering windows it hadn't taken much effort. Mackenzie knew better.

Candles burned everywhere. Red candles. Green candles. Milky white candles. Long slim tapers were surrounded by holly and pinecones. Tiny votives floated in cranberry-studded crystal bowls. Thick, slow-burning house warmers were trimmed with ribbons and bells. Their soft light flickered in every windowsill, on the low accent tables and across the evergreen-draped mantel that was to be their altar.

The cabin was redolent with the scent of hot, spiced cider, cinnamon and evergreen. Poinsettias—vibrant red, mottled pink, speckled white—graced each step of the loft stairs and joined the candles on the mantel.

Yesterday, J.D., Mark and Casey had trooped into the woods, searched for and found the perfect Christmas tree, which they'd cut down and dragged home with the help of the team of Belgian horses.

Over twelve feet tall, the tree sat regally in a prominent corner of the living room, adorned in twinkling lights, glittering garland and sparkling ornaments that Scarlett had generously shared from the supply she used to decorate the rooms in the Crimson Falls Hotel.

The overall effect was beautiful. And remarkably, Mackenzie actually felt that she was worthy of being a part of the picture. She caught her reflection in the tall living room windows as she emerged from the bedroom and hall...and allowed herself a secret smile.

With Maggie and Scarlett's enthusiastic assistance, she'd been transformed from plain Mackenzie Jane Kincaid into a passably acceptable bride.

When Maggie had insisted on taking her to town to shop for a dress yesterday, Mackenzie had been in a quandary about how to tell her that she didn't have the money. Finally she'd just blurted it out.

"Not a problem," Maggie had said easily, and bundled her into their four-wheel-drive Jeep and peeled out of the lane. "Abel said to get you anything you needed and he'd take care of it."

She'd had to chew on that for a while, but finally decided she wouldn't fight it. Abel had said he'd provide for her. He was simply keeping his word. She felt even better when Maggie added, "He knows this is awkward for you, and he wants to make it as pleasant as possible."

Pleasant didn't begin to describe how she felt, dressed in the emerald green wedding dress. *Glowing* came closer, though she would never before have thought in a million millennia that that adjective could ever apply to her.

True, it wasn't the traditional white silk and lace. But then this wasn't a traditional wedding.

They'd already purchased her new coat when her gaze

had snagged and held on the silky soft wool crepe in a surprisingly upscale dress shop in Bordertown.

"Try it on," Maggie had suggested with an encouraging smile.

When she'd stepped self-consciously out of the dressing room and was met by Maggie's sparkling eyes and her adamantly whispered "Yes," she knew she'd made her choice.

Mackenzie touched a hand to her hair, which Scarlett's clever hands had fluffed and styled. Delicate sprigs of baby's breath—an impromptu offering from Casey—had been tucked artfully among the soft curls in place of a veil.

Smiling at the whimsical effect, she trailed her hand down to the softness of the gently draping drop neckline of the dress. The sleeves were long, drifting over the backs of her hands in soft folds to mirror the neckline. The skirt fell away in flowing lines across her hips, ending midway between her knee and ankle.

She'd never felt so feminine or so vulnerable, she realized, as she pried her gaze away from her image to meet the dark, unreadable eyes of her bridegroom.

Her breath caught. Her chest filled. Her heart erupted as she took in the sight of him standing there.

She'd seen him savage. She'd seen him sullen. She'd never seen him tamed. A suit—as dark as the hair he'd tied at his nape with a thin black ribbon—both confined and defined the hard edges of his warrior's body. His civilized white shirt only served to emphasize the stunning contrast of his bronze skin against it.

But it was his eyes that relayed the true measure of the man waiting for her at the altar. Behind those eyes was a man of honor. A kind and caring man, who needed her to help him find the way.

His eyes weren't fooling her any longer. Once, she'd

thought they were unreadable. They spoke volumes to her today. And what they said made her heart sing with hope.

Clutching her bouquet of holly berries, winter white carnations and red roses, she walked unerringly toward him.

Oblivious to anything but the man waiting for her, she passed J.D. and Maggie where they stood sharing a loose embrace and soft, indulgent smiles. Unaware of Scarlett's and Casey's grins as she passed, she approached the altar. Cognizant of Mark's searching gaze, she reassured him with a quick smile and slipped to Abel's side.

He took her hand. And though she hadn't been prepared to, she gave him her heart.

In a blur of velvet black eyes, flickering candles and murmured responses, Mackenzie Kincaid became Mrs. Abel Greene.

In a marathon of champagne toasts, warm hugs and laughing congratulations, she was enveloped in his circle of friends.

And finally, in a haze of nervous anticipation, she watched as J.D. and Maggie, along with the minister, pulled out of the snow-packed lane.

"You don't have to worry about Mark."

Abel's dark eyes were hooded as he watched her face.

Scarlett and Casey had left just ahead of the Hazzards. Insisting that the newlyweds needed some time alone, they'd taken Mark to the hotel with them to spend the next few days.

"This time of year we've got more empty rooms than J.D. has one-liners," Scarlett had said, grinning as J.D. made a stab at looking wounded. "School's out until after Christmas vacation, so Casey will be at loose ends, anyway. She can show Mark the lake—maybe even introduce him to some of her friends so he won't start the semester completely in the dark."

Mackenzie had recognized Mark's initial response as what he'd felt was an obligatory grumble—and maybe a little protective concern for her—before he'd shrugged and mumbled, "Whatever."

"I'm not worried about him." She turned back to the window. "I'm a little concerned for Scarlett and Casey, though," she added with a small smile.

"They can handle him."

But can I handle you? she wondered. She wished she didn't feel so skittish as her husband loosened his tie and tugged it slowly from his collar.

Her husband.

The prewedding jitters had just kicked in—and only about two hours too late, she thought with irony. *Story of my life.*

For all of her earlier confidence, the reality of being married to this man finally sank in. He'd seen to everything with a quiet confidence and authority—from acquiring the marriage license to selecting the ring she now wore. She hugged her fingers around the solid gold band, stroked its shining warmth and knew that the identical ring he wore held the heat of his body, too.

Suddenly she didn't know what to do with her eyes, or her hands, or for that matter with herself.

Aware that he was watching her, she walked on stiff legs to the fire, drawing on its hypnotizing warmth to sooth her.

"I'm not going to jump you."

The darkness in his voice startled her. His eyes were even darker when she whirled around to search his face.

Breathless, she watched him drape his tie over the back of a chair and loosen the top two buttons of his shirt.

"It...it didn't occur to me that you would."

In truth, she hadn't let herself think about this moment. When she'd pictured them together—and she had, numerous times—they'd been far beyond this preliminary dance where all the right steps seemed to elude her.

In her fantasies, she'd said "I do." *The camera faded to black. Next scene: Soft light. Flickering candles. Big bed. A man and a woman entwined in each other's arms—naked, needy and with carnal knowledge of all the secrets and pleasures she'd been so anxious to learn.*

"Would you like some more champagne? J.D. would be disappointed if he thought it was going to waste."

She forced a smile and told herself to settle down. "He was pretty proud of himself for finding it."

He nodded. "A resourceful man."

"And a good friend," she prompted, searching for some level ground, when each step felt like an uphill climb.

The silence lengthened, and she realized he was still watching and waiting for her answer.

The problem was, she'd forgotten the question.

He lifted the bottle. Tilted his head.

"Oh. Sure. If you're having some."

He considered, then poured them each a glass.

Walking slowly to the fire beside her, he extended the sparkling champagne.

With a trembling hand she lifted it to her mouth, then almost dropped the glass when he said her name.

"Mackenzie."

His voice was as soft as the candlelight. Her name on his tongue like a velvet caress.

"The dress is nice. It matches your eyes."

His words surprised her so, she felt a flush that had nothing to do with the fire's heat spread across her cheeks.

Where was her smart mouth when she needed it? Mackenzie Kincaid, who had a one-liner for everything, couldn't think of a single thing to say, while Abel Greene who spoke only when provoked, seemed to have no such problem now.

"You look very pretty today."

The man was a complete and total enigma. He claimed he was incapable of emotions, but he knew how to melt her heart with pretty words and haunted eyes. And a solid gold band.

She lowered her lashes and groped for composure.

"Is it that hard...accepting a compliment from me?"

The edge in his voice brought her head up. The look on his face gave her pause.

"No. Oh, no," she said quickly. "I just...I didn't expect it. And the truth is...I haven't had much practice fielding...compliments."

Embarrassed by the wistfulness of her confession, she felt herself flush again. She took a long sip of champagne, then, prompted by the protracted silence, braved a glance his way.

She lifted a shoulder in a self-conscious little shrug. "I've never thought of myself as pretty."

Exposing her fears and her feelings to a man who professed to have none heightened her sense of vulnerability.

"Thank you," she said belatedly, then gave in to the demands of her pride. "But you didn't have to say it. In case it's slipped your mind..." She held up her left hand reminding him of the solid gold band on her ring finger. "I'm a sure thing."

He didn't say anything as she stood there embarrassed by her smart mouth and feeling more exposed by the moment. Instead, he touched a hand to her hair and gently tugged a sprig of baby's breath free.

"As you've pointed out," he said, studying the tiny white flowers that looked even smaller and more delicate in his big hand. "I'm a man of few words. I don't waste them on statements I don't mean."

His words couldn't have been more effective if he'd told her she was the most beautiful woman in the world. Something inside Mackenzie's breast throbbed to an awakening fullness, a rich, consuming confidence.

He thought she was pretty. For herself, as well as for him, she wanted to think so, too.

"Are you a virgin, Mackenzie?"

She hadn't thought he could shock her again. At least not this soon. Once past it, she considered his question logically. It was frank and it was necessary.

"I'm not a virgin. But my...relationships have been minimal. I...I've been careful. You don't have to worry about—"

The gentle pressure of his thumb on her lips stopped more than her explanation. Her heart quit beating. Her breath evaporated.

"That wasn't my concern."

"No?" she whispered, the sound more sigh than substance.

"No."

The touch of his hand, the scent and heat of his skin, filled her with a blistering awareness and an aching need.

"My concern was for your experience—or lack of it. I don't want to hurt you."

Abel saw the moment when the full implication of his statements finally dawned on her. She knew she'd been found out. And those telling eyes of hers relayed that she was hovering somewhere between mortification and relief.

If he'd had a sense of humor, he would have smiled. If he'd had a heart, it would have melted.

She'd thought she'd passed herself off as a woman of experience that morning in his kitchen. She'd coiled onto his lap like a kitten begging to be petted—and she'd been scared down to her pretty bare toes the entire time.

Not that she hadn't accomplished what she'd set out to do. She'd definitely seduced him. But not with her sexual prowess or experience. It was her innocence that had done him in. The tremble of her hands against his skin, the quickening of her breath when she'd dared press herself against him. The thrumming of her pulse when he'd taken the kiss she'd offered.

He'd ached for her ever since. One taste of her sweet, inexperienced mouth had left him hungry and hard and knowing he could show her much of the art of physical love.

While an emotional involvement was beyond him, a physical one was not. He regretted that he couldn't give her the commitment he knew she wanted...but he had every intention of giving her pleasure.

"Come," was all he said—was all he trusted himself to say—as he took her hand in his and led her to his bed.

Dusk came early to the lake land in December. It was barely five o'clock, yet soft shadows danced through the west window of his bedroom. The sun, a brilliant magenta disk, surrendered the day by painting the sky a mottled red and casting a rosy, translucent glow over the darkening room...and the man who stood watchful and waiting before her.

She'd known he would be beautiful. Even before he'd slipped out of his jacket and freed the buttons on his shirt, she'd known the skin beneath would be smooth and golden, the flesh it covered fluid and generously muscled.

What she hadn't known was that her desire for him would outdistance her reservations. She'd lost her heart when he'd taken her hand at the altar. She'd lost her inhibitions when he'd told her she was pretty and led her to his bed.

It shouldn't be like this. She shouldn't feel like this. She knew so little of him, really. What she did know should have filled her with reservations. He'd minced no words when he'd told her she was letting herself in for heartache if she expected more than a physical relationship. But she could no more sever her emotions from her desires than the tide could deny it was pulled by the moon.

She couldn't stop herself. When she reached out to this man who asked for and offered nothing more than the physical side of love, she reached with her heart as well as her hand.

There was no hesitance in her touch. No thought that he would deny her. She spread her fingers wide over the sculptured breadth of his bicep as he slipped out of his shirt and tossed it to the floor. Her hand looked small and pale, an erotic, hypnotic contrast to the bronze skin it caressed with a slow, tantalizing exploration.

With a thready breath, she brought her hands to his shoulders. Silk over steel. Hot to the touch. The tension in his finely honed body was drawn as tight as the anticipation that was knotted in her breast.

What would he be like, her savage, sullen lover? What would he do with all that strength? All that power?

She closed her eyes when he lowered the zipper on her dress. Pressed her hands against his chest to steady herself. The warmth of his breath feathered across the top of her head. His deep voice rumbled beneath her palms.

"You're not afraid?"

She was many things at this moment. Restless. Yearning. Needy. But the only thing she was afraid of was that she would die of this fierce desire to make love to him.

First she told him. "I'm not afraid."

Then she showed him.

Slipping her arms free of her dress, she let it slide down her hips and pool at her feet on the floor.

He went deadly still. Only his eyes touched her, awakening every pulse point, arousing every sensitive secret spot that ached for the caress of his hands, the warm, wet heat of his mouth.

"You give your trust too easily."

With a trembling hand, she trailed her fingertips along the proud, defiant rise of his cheek. "I give it where I know it's safe."

His eyes darkened, denial and warning tangled with desire.

"I know the parameters." Her voice was barely a breath that rustled the tension in the room. "This isn't about expectations. This is about choices. *My* choices. It has nothing to do with yours. I want to trust you. I know that I can."

He looked past her to the fading blush of the twilight sky. She sensed the battle he was waging even before he said the words.

"I don't want to hurt you, Mackenzie."

He wasn't speaking about physical hurt. He was talking about another kind of pain. One he knew about well, and which kept him from offering anything more than the comforts of his home and the pleasures of the flesh.

"I know."

Despite his words, she was aware of the need in him and it fired a new urgency to complete the act that would bind them together as husband and wife.

"Will you kiss me, Abel?" she whispered, desperate suddenly. "Will you kiss me…like that morning in the kitchen?"

Slowly he raised his hands to her hair. Gently he cupped her face in his palms. His eyes were open, searching as he stroked the underside of her jaw with his long fingers. His mouth was seeking as he slowly lowered his head.

The first touch of his lips to hers was more whisper than contact. More promise than pressure. Much more give than take.

Yet he took her breath away.

She clasped her fingers around his wrists to draw him closer. He wouldn't give her closer. He gave her temptation instead. He gave her the sweetest kind of torment, leaving her breathless and whispering his name.

His mouth was incredibly tender, achingly seductive, as his tongue flirted at the seam of her lips, allowing only a taste of what she wanted, only a hint of what was yet to be.

He played his mouth across hers. A gentle nip. A silken sip. An agonizing withdrawal. Each touch enticed her higher. Each lazy thrust of his tongue pledged a promise and left her wanting more.

"Please...please," she murmured then knotted her hands in his hair and begged him to take her deep.

His desire became a dark thing then. His passion went far beyond need. She felt it in the crush of the arms that enfolded her, in the taste of the mouth that finally claimed and possessed. And she wanted it all. Every groaning sound of hunger. Every urgent breath of greed.

His kisses consumed her. He tasted of champagne and danger and wants she could only imagine. She drowned in the heat of his mouth and sweet savage demands of his body.

His hands were everywhere. Pressing and pulsing along the length of her back. Possessing as they claimed her hips and ground her against the hard length of his arousal.

She caught her breath on a gasp as he suddenly lifted her in his arms and urged her legs around his waist. The heat of his bare chest seeped through the satin of her slip. His fingers burned with the fire of banked passion as they tunneled under the edge of her panties and drew her to more intimate contact.

Where she should have felt vulnerable, she felt only need. And desire. She squirmed against him, wanting more of the big hands that kneaded her bottom, the rough fingers that squeezed, then petted, then sought that part of her that was already wet, already swollen and ready for him.

She sighed into his mouth, swallowed his ragged groan when he touched her there. Boldly. Deeply. His caress was electric. His knowledge of how to please her carnal and unrelenting.

So fast, so fierce, the pleasure came. So fast it scared her. So fierce a cry escaped. A wild sound. A wanton plea, ripe with wonder, raw with passion. Breathless, she arched against his hand, then clutched his shoulders and cried his name as the first wave of a shattering orgasm took her.

Searing heat consumed her, spiraling from the source of the flame he'd ignited to the deepest core of her body. She clung to him, riding out the exquisite sensations until she collapsed bonelessly against him, her heart exploding, her mouth open against his chest.

She'd never known it could be like this. She'd never known the world could cease to exist. That one moment in time could be the only moment, blinding, golden and glowing.

She'd never known she could feel so totally and completely indulged.

"Thank you," she whispered against his shoulder and felt a teardrop fall.

Abel held her close against him. He felt the warm trickle of her tears on his skin, and the fullness in his chest grew heavier. He was no stranger to pleasing women. He'd even been thanked before. But never with such wonder and such sweet, aching innocence. And never had he taken such pleasure in the giving.

Even as she rested, sated and limp against him, she had no idea what her wanton response had done to him. She had no idea of the things he wanted to do with her still.

The silk of her slip sighed against his hands as he shifted her slight weight and laid her back on his bed. He wanted far more than satisfaction now. He wanted to ease that gnawing, unfamiliar ache that had been knotting in his chest ever since she'd pledged him her life.

He clenched his jaw against the rush of tenderness her faith in him fostered. He didn't understand it. And he sure as hell hadn't earned it. But it was there in a pair of trusting green eyes, now heavy-lidded with latent passion, and a heart riding in full view on her sleeve.

She made him want things that weren't possible. She made him want to let down his guard. To indulge. Not only in her body, but in her spirit and the warmth of the trust she offered as she lay there, so innocently seductive in the pristine white slip his hands had tangled around her hips.

He'd told her she was pretty. She'd made him feel like he'd given her a gift. A new experience for a man who had always been a taker. An unsettling catharsis for a man who'd never wanted to share anything more complicated than sex with a woman. That's all he'd ever been capable of sharing—a physical joining, mutual satisfaction the only requirement.

Yet with this woman who was now his wife, he'd found himself wanting to give.

He watched her face as he stripped off the last of his clothes and eased onto his hip beside her.

"You are a beautiful man, Abel Greene." Her whisper was as soft as the fading remnants of sunlight dappling the pillow where her head lay.

He'd known she had the power to arouse him. He hadn't known she could embarrass him. He trailed a finger along the deep vee of the white satin skin between her breasts. "I've been called a number of things in my life. Beautiful isn't one of them."

She smiled, catlike and content. "Then I'm glad the first time you heard it was from me." Shy suddenly, she raised a hand to his hair. "Will you untie it for me?"

She was a study in contrasts. She gave praise easily but

was uncomfortable accepting it. She offered generously but hesitated to ask if she could take.

That would be her first lesson. He'd teach his little bird to take what she wanted in this bed.

"You'll untie it," he said, "whenever you decide you want to."

He brought her hand to his mouth. Her skin was silky soft, like her hair, like the breath that escaped when he eased a finger beneath the strap of her slip and slowly tugged it down her arm.

Heat and hunger arrowed to his groin with each pale inch of flesh he exposed. Her breasts were small, her nipples tight and hard against the fabric that now barely covered a delicate, distended tip.

He was a big man, and he hadn't been with a woman for a very long time. She was a small woman and she was fragile, despite her determination to show him otherwise.

"Tell me," he began, his voice raspy with the effort of self-control, "tell me if I go too fast for you."

She told him instead what she wanted. Not in words. With a sensuous lift of her shoulder that sent the second strap slipping down her arm to bare the lush curve of her other breast; with a flirtatious lift of her hips as she shoved down her panties.

Suppressing a groan, he reminded himself to go easy with her. But looking wasn't enough anymore. Neither was merely touching. He remembered the taste of her. Remembered the feel of her in his mouth that morning when he'd stolen a sip of a pale, pink breast. The memory demanded. The reality beckoned.

Easing down on an elbow, he lowered his mouth to the hollow of her throat, then lost himself in her fragrance and the entreaty of her throaty sigh.

She smelled of strawberries and cream and innocence. And of the heady scent of a well-pleased woman.

She didn't know what she was doing to him. She didn't understand that when she wrapped her arms around his neck and moved against him with a restless urgency, she was blowing his good intentions all to hell.

He'd wanted to make this slow for her. *Slow* was beyond him now. With a hand made rough by anticipation, he stripped the thin barrier of satin to her waist and possessed her breast with his callused palm. She arched into his touch, filling his hand with heat and softness and a delicious quivering anticipation. He brushed his thumb across the velvet peak, sucked in a breath at her trembling response, then took her deep into his mouth.

Sin had never tasted this sweet. Sex had never been this seductive. He told himself it was because of his abstinence. He told himself it was because he'd lived too many years without giving in to his needs.

But then she took him in her hand and he knew it was *she* who had the power to make his heart stop beating. His breath clogged in his throat, then eased out on a long, shuddering groan when, with a hesitant, untutored caress, she explored and tortured and drove him to a new level of desperation.

He grew rigidly still above her, fighting for control, holding himself together by a tether no stronger than a length of silk thread.

"Make me your wife," she murmured, and lifted her hands to his hair. With her eyes holding his, she tugged the black ribbon free. His hair spilled over his shoulders, pooled in black drifts across the rosy tips of her breasts.

She threaded it through her fingers, caressing its length with a lover's touch. Bringing a handful to her face, she closed her eyes and breathed in its scent.

"Make me your wife," she said again, her green eyes dark and dancing as she pulled him down. Down into her heat. Deep into her arms and made a place for him between her thighs.

He hadn't known he'd been beaten. He hadn't guessed that a woman so small could destroy his will with whispered words and a silken touch.

She had the strength now. She had the power. He surrendered to it willingly. Gave it over with a long, slow stroke...and discovered the exquisite, searing pleasure of defeat.

On a sharp, indrawn breath she arched against him, welcoming him home, taking him deep, as he buried himself in sleek, wet heat and tight, clenching muscle. He ceased to exist past the feel of her. She was liquid fire surrounding him. She was shivery sighs and soft, trembling flesh beneath him.

If he could stay inside her forever, it wouldn't be long enough. His fear was that if he withdrew he'd find out it was all a dream. But then she moved beneath him. She sighed his name, whispered a lover's plea. And he was lost.

He pumped once, twice, and with an oath of denial, gave in to the rush that came far too soon. His climax was violent. Consuming. Complete. He rocked his hips against hers, extending the pleasure, deepening the contact to the sound of her own stunned cry of release, the taste of her on his tongue and the clutch of her fingers in his hair.

Eight

Long after he'd rolled to his back and away from her, long after he'd drifted into a sprawling, sated sleep, Mackenzie lay in his bed and watched the moonlight dancing through the window.

A hundred feelings feathered and floated around in her head, competing for and tangling with a delicious sense of weightless suspension. Excitement. Embarrassment. Wonder. Elation. She turned her head on the pillow and watched her husband sleep.

Love.

Hope.

He was wrong. He was *so* wrong. She *didn't* give her trust too easily. And he wasn't immune to the urgings of his heart. He couldn't have made love to her so sweetly, with such exquisite attention to her needs, if he didn't care.

She felt herself flush with the remembered heat, the intimate touch of his hands and his mouth. Her gaze strayed to his powerfully muscled body—to that part of him that was covered by a drift of white sheet and moonlight—and she wanted him again. The strength of her need stunned her.

She'd never thought of herself as a sensual person. And she'd never dreamed she could have given herself so wantonly to any man. But Abel Greene wasn't any man. He was *her* man, and she was going to do everything in her power to take care of the needs of his heart—just as she intended to take care of the needs of his body.

She wasn't going to have the strength to accomplish either, though, if she didn't get something to eat. She needed nourishment. Soon. She'd been too jittery to eat much of the wonderful wedding feast Scarlett and Maggie had prepared, and the toast and coffee she'd had for breakfast that morning had worn off long ago.

Easing carefully out of bed so she wouldn't wake him, she grabbed the first thing within reach and shrugged it on, then hugged it to her face and breathed in the essence of Abel Greene. His discarded white dress shirt was scented of him—it even felt like him, big and substantial and sensually rough against her bare skin.

She rolled up the cuffs as she shuffled out of the room, then fastened a few buttons on the way to the fireplace. Soft fire glow lit the room, accompanying the flicker of the candles that still burned and scented the cabin with cinnamon, bayberry and vanilla.

Mimicking the actions she'd seen Abel do dozens of times since she'd been here, she opened the mesh screen covering the fire, hefted a piece of birch and settled it on the grate. Then she stood back and smiled when the flames licked and caught hold.

"I think you've got the hang of it, Mackenzie Greene," she said, pleased with herself, pleased with the sound of her new name as she closed the screen, brushed off her hands and padded into the kitchen.

The wedding cake on the counter beckoned. She flicked on the light over the sink, casting the kitchen in more shadow than light, and hunted up a knife. Suddenly she was ravenous. She didn't bother with a plate or fork. She sliced a piece of the richly frosted white sheet cake, picked it up with her fingers and brought it to her mouth.

That's how her husband found her.

The overhead light blinked on, startling her. She whirled around, her mouth full of cake, her fingers covered in frosting and her heart in her throat.

He stood just inside the room, arms crossed over his bare chest, a broad shoulder propped against the wall. The jeans he'd pulled on rode low on his hips, the zipper at half-mast. He was barefoot and she would bet her last penny, bare beneath those jeans.

And he was the most extraordinarily beautiful man she'd ever seen.

In contrast, she was excruciatingly aware that standing there in his shirt, her hair wild and bed mussed, she must look about as provocative as a grocery sack.

She swallowed a mouthful of cake, then gave him a sheepish smile.

"I got hungry," she confessed, stating the obvious with a self-conscious little shrug that sent his shirt slipping off one shoulder.

He just stood there, his black eyes taking a slow, thorough inventory, starting with her bare toes and crawling unhurriedly up the length of her body before finally landing on her face.

The fire in his eyes was unmistakable. She felt an answering flame, amazed that she could look like this and he could still want her.

"Would you...like some..." Her voice trailed off as he

walked unerringly toward her. "Cake?" she finally managed to say.

Then she exhaled on a thready little breath at his murmured "Please."

Spellbound by the look in his eyes, she stood motionless, sexual tension vibrating between them.

"You said something about cake." His voice was so soft it took her a moment to realize she hadn't imagined it.

"Right. Cake."

With her heart hammering, she turned back to the counter to cut him a slice—only to have him snag her wrist and turn her around to face him.

"No." His slumberous gaze dropped to the cake she held in her fingers. "This is the piece I want."

She stopped breathing. His voice was so deep. So drugging. So impossible to deny, as he drew her hand and the half-eaten piece of cake slowly toward him.

She thought she'd known anticipation. She thought she'd understood seduction—then he taught her new meanings of both. With his eyes holding hers captive, he brought her hand to his mouth, drew both the cake and her fingers inside.

Her knees turned to noodles as he lavishly and lazily licked the icing from her fingers, then treated her palm to the same lush strokes of his tongue. His eyes turned stormy and dark as he pressed her open hand to his face and bit the fleshy part of her thumb.

Thunder rumbled through her blood as he kissed the little sting away. Lightning sizzled through her body as he lowered his hands to her waist, lifted her and set her on the counter.

The countertop was cold beneath her bare bottom. The heat in his eyes warmed her as he lowered his head to hers. Instead of the kiss she yearned for, he made a pleasured sound deep in his throat and licked a dollop of frosting from the corner of her mouth.

"You're very sweet," he murmured, his breath whispering against her lips. "And very messy."

She swallowed and felt herself melting as his tongue flicked out again, playing with the seam of her lips, eating at the corners of her mouth like she was a piece of candy and he was the kid who'd discovered the candy store.

"I think I'll have some more."

Arousal built like a summer storm as he glanced down at the cake, scooped a fingerful of frosting and brought it to his mouth.

His eyes locked on her face, he slowly licked his finger, taking a long, considering taste.

Desire knotted in her breast then unraveled in a sharp, arching rush as she watched the slow strokes of his tongue, mesmerized, electrified.

"Good." His voice was a rough, sultry whisper that drew her eyes to his. "But I like it better on you."

Sweet lord, he was going to tease her to death. She gripped the edge of the counter with trembling fingers, as with carnal attention to the play of his hands, he smeared the icing from her chin to her bare shoulder.

She didn't have the will to suppress a shudder when his mouth followed the trail of his finger. Like a gourmet sampling French pastries, he savored and sipped and licked his way down her throat, across the rise of her collarbone and, with a combination of lips and teeth and tongue, glided over the length of her bared shoulder.

She whimpered when he lifted his head, let her head fall back against the cupboard door as his hands rose and freed the buttons on the shirt she wore. With tantalizing attention to each inch of flesh he revealed, he peeled it down her arms, exposing her breasts to his slumberous gaze.

"I seem to have developed an insatiable taste for... frosting."

The explicit intent of his rumbled words sent her entire body into sexual overload. Her nipples were diamond hard and tugging at places deep and low even before he laved them with frosting, then drew each one alternately into his mouth.

Sweet, sharp pleasure engulfed her as he suckled and nuzzled and feasted. Desire clawed at her as she cradled his head to her breast and begged him to set her free.

His control broke the same time hers did. With a guttural oath, he scooped her roughly off the counter and laid her on her back on the table. She reached for him, lifting her hips as he moved between her legs, freed himself from his jeans and entered her in a swift, hard thrust.

She cried his name. He swore hers and gripped her hips, tilting her to better receive him...again...again...again.

Each thrust took her higher, until she was no longer aware of the table, cool and hard beneath her back, the kitchen light, harsh and bright in her eyes. She was only aware of him, and that awareness consumed her. He was magnificently aroused. Aggressively male. His eyes were closed. His head thrown back, the cords on his neck distended and glistening with perspiration. His hair trailed down his back like a spill of black ink as he set a rhythm as savage as the warrior he resembled and as abandoned as the erotic thrill of their joining.

In a blinding rush he transported her to that exquisite peak where sensation dominated and passion ruled. And where love for this man could not be denied.

His little bird looked broken. Damning himself for an animal, Abel reluctantly withdrew from the sweet, tight haven of her body. He tugged up his jeans and zipped them, then leaned over the table to assess the damage.

Her eyes were closed. Her arms limp, her palms upturned where they lay on the table by her head. He bit back another oath when he saw the delicate flesh of her breasts reddened and swollen from his rough treatment.

"Did I hurt you bad, green eyes?"

Her eyes fluttered open. Her kiss-swollen lips lifted in a sultry little smile. "You hurt me good...so good," she murmured and let her eyes drift shut again. "I don't believe I've ever known anyone who enjoyed frosting as much as you do."

He told himself it was relief that let the small smile get away from him. Then he reined it in, reminding himself that no matter what she said, he'd treated her badly.

"Don't move," he ordered as he left the kitchen to get a blanket, suppressing another smile at her mumbled "Don't worry."

He hadn't intended to attack her. He'd woken, found her gone and gone looking for her. He wasn't entirely insensitive. His concern had been that she might be feeling self-conscious about their lovemaking. He'd wanted to offer some assurance that she'd pleased him—and to assure himself that he hadn't been too rough with her.

Instead of finding a timid and contemplative little sparrow, he'd found a summer bird in full feather. And he'd been blown away. Everything about the look of her—from her tiny bare feet to her tousled hair, still studded with wisps of crushed baby's breath, to the sight of his shirt covering her to her knees and trailing provocatively off one shoulder—had tempted him to steal another kiss, induce a shivery sigh.

It wasn't supposed to have gone any further than that. He'd just wanted a kiss. Just a promise of more pleasure, until after she'd rested and he'd gotten himself under control. But a kiss hadn't been enough.

She'd been incredible. An intoxicating blend of wide-eyed innocence and pagan seduction.

When he returned to the kitchen with the blanket, the pleasure of seeing her in all her pink, naked glory almost waylaid his resolve to back off and let her be. With a grim set of his mouth and a determination to see to her needs, he eased her up, bundled her in the blanket, then carried her to the sofa in front of the fire.

"Don't go." Her voice was small, her eyes soulful when he'd turned toward the kitchen.

"I'll be right back," he assured her, troubled but not surprised by his need to reassure her. "You need something to eat."

Her eyes narrowed, then glistened with a sweet, seductive fire.

"Something more substantial than cake," he added, and got the hell out of there before he gave in to the temptation to unwrap her and take her one more time.

She ate with the enthusiasm of a lumberjack. Either he'd never noticed or she'd kept herself in polite control until now. She dug into the sandwich he'd made her like she hadn't eaten in a week—or like a woman who'd lost more than her sexual inhibitions.

He'd never dreamed she'd be such a delicious little wanton. And he'd never factored in this insatiable need to make love to her.

He didn't want to explore the reasons why. He sure as hell didn't want to dwell on them. He wasn't a kid whose hormones led him around. He was a man who prided himself on his control.

And she was a woman who had the ability to strip that control to the bone.

He glanced at the clock. And swore. It was barely seven o'clock. There was a lot of darkness left in this night. And a lot of woman on his sofa, willing to let him take advantage of it and her. He couldn't let it keep happening. He hadn't hurt her yet, but if he gave in to every erotic craving she brought out in him, they'd both be in need of medical attention by morning.

He had to get away from her. Or at least get them both out of the cabin. The last thought sounded far better than the first.

"Are you up for a little exercise?" he asked, when she'd polished off the last of her sandwich.

Her head came up. She flushed, then gave him a sassy little grin he had a hard time keeping himself from answering.

"I'll rephrase. Are you up for a little outside exercise—and some fresh air?"

She toned down her smile, cast a glance toward the windows. "It's dark out there."

He rose, taking her plate with him. "Not that dark. The moon is full. There's plenty of light."

She considered, then shrugged. "Sure. Why not."

He took one last look at her, all rosy and dewy soft and undeniably tempting and set his jaw. "Go ahead and get dressed while I let Nashata out and check on the pups."

Mackenzie felt foxy and female and invincible. Even though she recognized that lust was a far cry from love, equal measures of both stirred her as she walked out of the cabin and into the December moonlight beside her husband.

He was right. The light was soft but plentiful. A big yellow moon hung low over the tops of the snow-laden pine forest. Shadows tumbled and shifted with a gentle winter wind. Starlight glittered with a brilliance unlike any she'd ever seen beneath the smog-clogged skies in the city.

She stopped. Shoved her hands deep in her pockets and stared in awe at the canvas of moonlight and star fire.

"It's...awesome," she managed finally.

He was quiet beside her, then surprised her by letting go of a piece of himself.

"I think this is what drew me back to the lake more than anything else. These quiet nights. The clarity. The silence so acute you can hear a snowflake fall."

"Were you gone a long time?" she asked softly, afraid to push, but afraid to lose the moment if she let this chance go by. She wanted to know. Why had he left? Why did he return? What made him so afraid to let someone in?

He started walking again. She fell in step beside him not knowing if her wait would yield an answer or more silence.

They reached the stable before he spoke. "I left here when I was eighteen. I decided to come back five years ago."

She wanted more, but decided to wait until he chose to give it freely. "Wise decision," she said, and answered his considering look with a soft smile.

He reset his expression in that mask he thought he'd perfected so well and opened the stable door. Flipping the light switch, he urged her in ahead of him.

The pair of black horses lolled contentedly in their open stalls. She'd known of their existence, had heard Mark jabber about the way they'd dragged the Christmas tree home the day she and Maggie had gone shopping, but she'd never seen them close up.

"They're huge," she said without preamble, struck by the size of them. "What on earth do you feed them?"

She watched from a distance as he snagged a flat, round brush from a peg on the wall. "Oats. Hay. A little corn in this cold weather to generate body heat," he said as he gave one of the horses a brisk brushing.

"So…what do they do…besides eat?"

He moved from one horse to the other. "Not much of anything. Occasionally I use them to drag logs when I can't get to them with the Cat. Other than that, I just like having them around.''

Hands stuffed in her pockets, she walked a little closer as he set aside the brush and gathered armfuls of leather straps and silver metal.

"What are you doing?"

"Bridling them."

A wave of unease rolled through her. "And you would be doing that because..." she ventured, afraid she already knew the answer.

He continued hooking and looping and walking around the horses' heads. "I would be doing that because I thought you might enjoy going for a ride."

What she might enjoy was trotting right back inside and burrowing under the covers in his big, soft bed. But she would eat some of that horse hay before she'd admit it. He was extending a gesture because he thought she would enjoy it—and she'd enjoy it if it killed her.

She looked up at the monster horses again and decided that *killed*, was, perhaps, not the best choice of words.

When he turned the pair around and led them by thick leather reins out the door, she jumped back until at Abel's urging, she inched over to stand beside one of the giants. It was even bigger up close.

"Not without a ladder, I won't," she blurted out before she could stop herself.

He cut her a look, then said in an even tone, "You don't need a ladder. Just reach up and grab a handful of her mane. Then put your foot in my hand and I'll give you a boost."

She stared from the patiently waiting man in front of her to the house disguised as a horse. "And the reason we aren't going to take this ride on a snowmobile is?" she prompted, hoping the mention of the snowmobile would inspire him into a change of plans.

"The reason is, so you can enjoy the night in relative quiet."

Before she could say "Noise is good," he circled her waist with his hands, lifted her high into the air and set her down on the horse's broad bare back.

She hadn't meant to scream. She wasn't even aware that she had until she found herself hanging on for dear life as a ton of rippling muscle and prancing hooves danced across the hard, snow-packed ground beneath her.

With a calming tone and gentle words, Abel steadied the skittish animal.

Eyes wide, Mackenzie clutched the mane like a lifeline and prayed she didn't get altitude sickness. "Not a good idea? The screaming, I mean?"

He shook his head, and—if her eyes weren't playing tricks on her—let the slightest hint of a smile tip up one corner of his mouth.

She forgot all about her fear then. She'd made Abel Greene smile. A first. A miracle. And it enhanced her sense of invincibility.

"Are we settled now, do you think?" he asked, one hand on the bridle, the other on the thick black winter coat of the draft horse's neck.

"Yes." The warmth of that unbelievable smile and the heat from the horse's body seeped through her clothes to take away the chill. "I think maybe we are."

Without another word he grabbed a handful of mane and swung effortlessly up on the other mare's back. After a quick glance her way to make sure she was steady, he nudged his horse into a slow walk. She was just beginning to wonder how to get hers going when it took a lumbering step forward and fell in step behind him.

"Are there brakes?" she asked Abel's broad back. "And not that I'm complaining, but aren't there supposed to be stirrups or something?"

He reined to a stop. Her horse plodded up beside its stablemate and stopped, too.

"This is just a wild guess," he ventured, a lightness in his voice she'd never heard before, "but is it possible you've never been horseback riding?"

"Not unless carousels count."

Again came that unexpected and breath-stealing whisper of a smile. "Not the last I knew."

"Then, no. This is a first for me. It's been a day full of firsts," she added before thinking, then made a great show of patting the horse's neck and smoothing its coarse thick mane so he wouldn't see her face redden at the thought of all the firsts she'd experienced—especially the ones he'd introduced her to in his bed.

"You can relax and enjoy the ride, Mackenzie," he said, misinterpreting embarrassment for hesitation. "She'll do all the work for you. And as long as you don't scream again, you're as safe as sitting in a rocking chair."

She looked from the horse to him. "She knows that, right?"

Gotcha again, she thought triumphantly as that magnificent mouth twitched again, then made a soft clucking sound that set both horses back in motion.

From that point on she did as he asked. She relaxed. She enjoyed—both the stark, snowy beauty of the forest and the company of the man at her side.

The woods were alive with whispered sounds and shadows of motion. She soon learned that when he stopped and pressed a finger to his lips it was her cue to follow his lead and sit very still. It wouldn't be long before a deer and her spring fawn would appear, all senses alert, ears twitching, noses to the wind before they tiptoed delicately across their path.

Night owls swooped, the wind stirred through their spread wings in a muffled shushing flutter. It was all so beautiful and foreign and new, like a world untouched by civilization, unmarred by progress. She hadn't expected to, but she loved every stolen, moon-kissed moment—just as she hadn't expected to love the man at her side.

She was so caught up in the pleasure of sharing this night with him that it took her a moment to realize the forest had disappeared.

"What happened to the trees?" she asked, as another marvel stretched out before her. A huge, empty expanse of nothing but white wavelike drifts had replaced the cocoon of snow-heavy pine and winter-barren birch.

"We've reached the lake."

The lake. She'd known it was close to his cabin, but she hadn't realized it would be so big or so starkly beautiful. It seemed to stretch on forever, mile upon mile of snow-capped ice bordered by forest, rock and wilderness.

"Legend Lake," she murmured, caught up in a sense of wonder and awareness of a history that was the source of myths and legends.

She looked at Abel. His large frame was enveloped in a heavy Mackinaw jacket, his arms crossed over the horse's withers as he surveyed the land he called home.

"Tell me a legend," she said softly.

His expression was pensive as he glanced at her, then averted his gaze out over the ice again. "My mother used to tell me stories," he said, his voice as reflective as his eyes. "Stories her grandmother and her mother before her had passed down."

Her silence prompted him for more.

"At the source of most of them was the legend of the Manabozho, the great wonder worker of the Chippewa. He is not only himself, my mother would say, but he can turn himself into all kinds of animal shapes."

"You make it sound like she believed in him."

He shrugged. "I think she wanted to believe—at least in the myth. In the magic."

"Do you remember any of her stories?"

She could see by the softening of his eyes that he did.

"Her favorite was the theft of fire."

"Tell me."

He shifted his weight, then began slowly. "Once, according to the legend, it was on this very shore that Manabozho's family suffered a bitter cold winter. The wind was brittle. The lake frozen deep. And the sun had lost all its heat."

He paused and she sensed that not only was he sifting through his memory for the words to the story, but to a place in his past he hadn't let himself visit in a very long time.

"When he asked his grandmother why it was so cold," he continued reflectively, "she told him that long ago the people had had heat within their wigwams but the fire had been stolen by a man who guarded it so no one else could have it. He told his grandmother he would find this man and bring back the fire. She said it couldn't be done, but he left, anyway, to search for it. He turned himself into an eagle and soared the lake until he spotted smoke coming from the top of a wigwam on a faraway shore. Then he turned himself into a rabbit and hopped inside the wigwam where the old man slept and there it was—the fire. He was excited but soon realized that even if he stole it, he didn't have any way to get it home. Then he came up with an idea."

"What?" she prompted, caught up in the fantasy of the fable and the pleasure in his voice. "What did he do?"

"He turned his backside to the flame until his big cotton tail caught fire. Then he hopped as fast as he could, his fur singed and burning, and collapsed in his grandmother's wigwam just before the last spark died. His grandmother fanned the flame, added tinder, and by the time Manabozho turned back into a boy, she had a warm fire burning in their lodge.''

"Which they shared with everyone and brought the warmth back into the sun," she suggested, her heart full of the sweetness of the legend and thoughts of Abel as a little boy sitting by his mother's side and begging her to tell the story again and again.

"Which they shared with everyone and brought the warmth back into the sun," he confirmed, and let his gaze drift across her face before turning back to the lake.

She felt the tenderness in his eyes long after he'd looked away. "It's a wonderful story."

"She was a remarkable woman." The reflective quality of his voice confirmed that this was a memory he hadn't let himself indulge in for a very long time.

She was a remarkable woman who had raised a young boy into a remarkable man, Mackenzie thought. Warmed by the events of the evening, but chilled suddenly by the coldness of the winter night. She hugged her arms around herself to stall a shiver.

He sent a concerned look her way. "You're cold."

She shook her head. "Maybe a little. I guess it'll take some more time for my body to acclimatize from California heat to Minnesota cold."

He didn't say anything. He just slid off the Belgian's back, walked to her side, then swung up behind her. Before she could figure out how he'd done it with such ease, he'd opened his coat and drawn her back against him. After bundling the coat around her, he took the reins from her hands and turned the horse back toward the cabin.

She snuggled willingly into his heat and the protective embrace of his arms around her. And like him, she surrendered to the silence that was accompanied only by the steady crunch of the horses' hooves digging into the snow and the whisper of his breath near her ear.

Are you dreaming? she asked herself, as the moon peeked through the outstretched arms of the trees, and the stars played peekaboo with their branches. The night and the man and what they had shared seemed surreal, suddenly, like they were a part of one of Manabozho's fables.

Here, blanketed by the night, enfolded in her husband's arms, it didn't seem possible that a mere week ago she'd been living in fear for her brother's life. And more. There'd been more that she hadn't wanted to admit to. More that she'd been struggling to overcome. She'd been tired. So very tired of always being the strong one, the one to fix things, to heal things, to right the wrongs she could no longer justify.

A week ago she'd been alone and defeated. And now she had moonlight and star glow and a savior by the name of Abel Greene.

Dream or reality. She no longer cared. She let the sense of security take her. At peace for the first time in a very long while, she fell asleep in the circle of his arms as the Belgian plodded steadily through the woods, her partner trailing along behind.

She woke up with a snuffling protest and burrowed closer to Abel's warmth.

"Mackenzie."

Soft breath tickled her cheek as a gentle hand tipped her face up.

"Wake up, little bird," Abel whispered in her ear. "You don't want to miss this."

What she didn't want to miss was the protective heat of his body.

"Come on," he urged, and gave her a little shake. "You'll be sorry if you don't wake up."

Grudgingly she dragged herself out of her cocoon and rubbed a gloved hand over her eyes.

"Look." He pointed toward the sky.

She caught her breath on an "Ohhh" of wonder. The night was aflame with color. Vibrant reds, glowing whites, myriad shades of green and ghostly hues of blue. Shimmering waves of rainbow tones danced in a jagged arc across the ceiling of sky that had come alive with a light show that stole her breath.

"What it is?" Fully awake now, she sat up straight, not knowing where to look first or next, afraid she might miss something.

"Aurora borealis. Northern lights."

It was another first for her. Another wonder in this land of legends and fables and ice.

"How...what causes it?"

"The scientific theory is that auroras are caused by clashes between the solar wind and the earth's magnetic field. Like a battle between the earth and sun."

"And the Chippewa theory?" she asked, eyes skyward.

"I'm not sure there is one."

"Well, I have one." She turned to look at him, averting her gaze from one thing of beauty to another. The light show reflected in his eyes as he gazed down at her.

"I think it's Manabozho. He turned himself into a spirit, and he's showing me with his magic colors how lucky I am to be here, at Legend Lake."

His face softened for the longest of moments before he broke eye contact and nudged the horse back into motion. "And I think it's time to get you out of the cold."

She snuggled back against him. He didn't realize it yet, but she'd come out of the cold the day she'd stumbled, half-frozen, to his door.

There was something else he didn't know. Just as Manabozho succeeded in stealing the fire, she was determined to melt the ice frozen around Abel's heart.

Nine

When the light show had faded and the night became even colder, Abel left her at the cabin, then headed back outside to bed down the horses. He needed the time away from her. Time to think and to put things back in perspective.

All was quiet when he slipped in the back door, telling him that she'd been exhausted and had tumbled into bed and fallen asleep.

Moving silently through the cabin, he fired up the sauna, then checked on Nashata. Satisfied that she and her brood were well settled, he stripped and showered. Wrapping a towel around his hips, he closed himself off in steam heat and solitude.

The sauna had been his biggest indulgence when he'd built the cabin. And his most necessary avenue for escape. When, in the dead of night, he'd wake with ghosts of his past chasing him, his heart hammering, his throat closed so tight he couldn't breathe, the sauna had been his refuge.

He could close himself in here. Surround himself with suf-focating, mind-numbing heat, and sweat the tremors away.

Tremors hadn't brought him here tonight. Neither had dreams of death and degradation. Mackenzie's vivid green eyes and the stark, unrelenting desire to possess her had driven him to sweat out his demons.

He leaned back against the wall, inhaled air thick with cedar and heat…and smelled only her. Her skin. Her hair. The secret scent of her arousal.

He closed his eyes…and saw only her. Frosting on her fingers. Seduction in her eyes. The pale suppleness of her slim hips in the brutal grip of his dark hands as she en-trusted her body to his keeping.

"Damn her," he growled, raking his hair away from his face with both hands. "What is she doing to me?"

He let out a deep breath. He knew exactly what she was doing. So did she. She was stealing his resolve. She was undermining his determination. She had him telling stories, for chrissake. Childhood stories that stirred memories and emotions he'd buried long ago.

He knew better. He knew the consequences of giving in. And still he wanted. He wanted to give in to his greatest weakness—the one that had been gnawing and clawing at him since he'd taken her to his bed and went far beyond physical desire.

She made him want to trust her. To disclose the secrets of his past, expose the atrocities, mourn the loss of his own innocence and the desolation and destruction of his soul.

Are you afraid? he'd asked her. A grim smile tightened his mouth. His little bird wasn't afraid of anything. But he was—he was so scared he ached with it.

His hands shook as he fisted them at his side. His breath thickened and clogged in his throat, as he struggled with the cloying fear of letting her too close—and the greater fear that he couldn't keep her close enough.

This was irony at its most bitter and vindictive best. If he gave her what she wanted—the confessions of his soul—the chances were he'd lose her. If he denied her, he'd lose himself and her along the way. A woman like her couldn't survive long in the cold, dark climate of his silence. A woman like her needed what he had never thought he could give—until she'd come into his life and knocked the props out from under him.

Make me your wife. In his mind he saw her as she'd looked when she'd lain beneath him, open, trusting, needing him as much as he'd needed the sweet sexual healing of her body.

Make me your wife. God she'd been sweet...as sweet as she looked at this moment, slipping tentatively into the steam-filled room.

His heart caught as had become habit whenever he saw her. His chest ached with a wanting that transcended physical need.

Midnight and moonlight washed in through the skylight, gilding the silken sheen of her skin as she stood there, fresh from a shower, a towel bunched between her breasts. Innocence and seduction. The combination was devastating. The intoxication complete.

He gave it up then. The pretense of distance. The denial of need. He'd been lost the first time he'd seen her. He just hadn't known it.

He held out his hand. And gave her his trust.

The words came hard. But they came, with gravel in his voice and a tightening in his gut.

"Make me your husband."

A new awareness clouded her eyes as they searched his—searched and sought and found the meaning of his words.

He'd given up. He'd given in. He'd given himself to her completely.

Tears glittered in her eyes, spilled down her cheeks, mingling with steam and perspiration as she let the towel fall and came to him.

"Again," she demanded with a soft voice he could no longer deny.

He looked deep into her eyes, saw the honesty of her heart and unashamedly confessed his need. "Make me your husband, Mackenzie." He swallowed the lump lodged in his throat. "I need—"

She pressed trembling fingers to his lips, silencing him.

"Shhh. I know what you need," she whispered, her skin glistening, her earth mother eyes knowing, her passion uninhibited and healing as she knelt beside him.

The knot at his hips gave way as she tugged the towel free then enfolded his heavy arousal in her hands. He lifted his hips, moved into her caress as she eased over his lap and with her eyes locked on his took him deep, so deep.

Steady and slow, she rocked against him, holding him inside, matching the rhythm he set, meeting the need she had created. She took him languidly, with the seductive confidence of a woman pleasuring her man, with her guileless smiles and her own throaty murmurs of pleasure.

There was no rush in this mating. There was no hurry now. They had forever, and they reveled in the freedom it offered.

When it was over and they'd collapsed together in a tangle of sweat-slicked limbs and thundering heartbeats, he held her against his heart. And for the first time in his life, he believed in magic.

Manabozho had stolen fire; Abel Greene had stolen something far more precious.

They stood together in the winter-barren cemetery. The sky overhead threatened snow, the color of the clouds promised wind.

Abel's mother was buried in a lonely corner away from the family plots and the city fathers. Mackenzie gripped his hand in hers as he dropped to one knee and brushed snow away from the austere, gray headstone.

"She was too young," Mackenzie said with a sadness in her voice that matched her husband's eyes, when she saw the date on the headstone.

"She was never young." His voice was as brittle as the wind, but his ability to confide his feelings warmed her like no summer sun ever could.

It had been three days since they'd been married. Three days that had changed her life as well as the life of the man at her side.

It wasn't easy for him. He took it very slowly. He'd given her little pieces of himself at first. Little pieces that didn't hurt and didn't reveal much more than surface blemishes. Little pieces that began to form and shape the intricate puzzle that was a picture of his life.

When he'd asked her to come here with him today, she'd suspected he was ready to breach yet another barrier.

"Your father," she said, hesitantly. "You haven't spoken of him."

He rose, dusted the snow from his hand and looked off in the distance. "Because he's not worth talking about. He was a drunk and a drifter, who never even bothered to marry my mother. He used her, abused her…" He paused, the tension on his face was telling. She had no doubt that he'd been a target for that abuse, too. She squeezed his hand and leaned into him.

In a gesture he never would have given in to even a day ago, he put his arm around her and tucked her against his side. "He bled her dry of her money and her pride and he left her. I haven't seen or heard from him since I was…I don't know…ten…maybe eleven."

"And you blame yourself for his leaving."

He gave her a sharp look, then shrugged. "Intellectually, no."

"But, emotionally," she prompted, leading him toward the anger she knew was bottled up inside.

"Emotionally—let's just say I understand Mark's anger. I reacted the same way he did when I was his age. I was Faye Greene's wild breed bastard. And I wanted to make damn sure everyone knew I was no good."

Mackenzie understood what else that had made him. The outsider. The loner who wouldn't have recognized a kindness extended because he was so busy blocking the fear of rejection with protective rage.

She hurt for the wounded little boy who now wore the scars as a man.

With a last look at his mother's grave, he turned to her. "There were many times, even before he left, that we went hungry. Many times when she could have sold the land and made her life easier. 'I have a faith to keep,' she would say. It was a faith she kept for me. And it's what drew me back to the lake.

"She left me the land, Mackenzie. The land that had belonged to the Chippewa and was entrusted to my family to keep. The land was the reason she worked two jobs. The land was the reason she fell asleep behind the wheel after working too late and too hard too often."

He stopped abruptly, stared at her hard. "There's a man. His name is Grunewald. John Grunewald."

"Grunewald." The sudden anger in his eyes frightened her. "Didn't I see his name on a sign somewhere?"

"He's the money man in town. Owns Grunewald-Castelle."

"The big paper mill."

He nodded. "He wants my timber. He's not going to get it."

His features had turned dark, his black eyes taking on a hardness she hadn't seen in days.

"Remember his name. And stay away from him. If he ever comes to the cabin when I'm not there—don't talk to him. Don't let him in. Don't listen to anything he has to say."

He gripped her shoulders and searched her face. "Promise me you won't let him near you."

"You make him sound like a monster." The smile she forced was meant to lighten a tension that was both uncomfortable and a little frightening.

"Promise me, Mackenzie," he demanded, his hands almost hurtful as he drew her closer. "Promise me you won't go anywhere near him."

"I promise," she whispered, unsettled by his adamant request, but choosing the path of least resistance. She wouldn't question him about Grunewald. Not today. Though the wounds his father had inflicted weren't completely healed, they were old wounds. Grunewald's damage was obviously fresher. And apparently he'd cut deep. "I promise," she assured him and leaned into his embrace.

He held her close for a long moment.

"Come on," he said finally, then walked her toward the pickup. "We need to go shopping. Mark will be coming home tomorrow. The kid needs a bed—even though he isn't complaining, he can't sleep in the loft forever."

The dream came that night.
Out of the void.
Out of the darkness.
He woke up thrashing, his chest heaving, his body drenched in sweat. Violent, clawing panic grabbed him, held him down, sucked him under. He broke free with an animal roar. Wrenching out of his assassin's grasp, he wres-

tled him to his back, wrapped his hands around his neck and squeezed away the life that had promised to take his.

From a distance he heard her cry. In a blur he sensed her near. He stilled, opened his eyes—and felt his heart drop to the lowest depths of his gut.

"No...oh, God, Mackenzie. No."

With a tortured groan, he dragged her against him, a prayer foreign but reverent on his tongue as he begged her and whatever powers that might be listening to let her be all right.

"Abel, please, stop fussing. I'm fine. I was more frightened than hurt."

"Which would explain why your throat is so sore you can hardly talk."

"You wish," she said, one corner of her mouth tipping up in a valiant smile, manufactured to set him at ease.

He didn't think he'd ever be at ease again. And he would feel guilt for the rest of his life for the way he'd hurt her.

She looked as wilted as a crushed flower. He'd brought her out of the bedroom and settled her on the sofa so he could tend to her needs. Already, angry-looking bruises were forming on her neck. The memory of waking up with her fighting for her life beneath him, his fingers wrapped in a choke hold around her throat, sent a wave of nausea rolling through him.

He rose from his knees, the thickness in his chest crushing him.

"Abel," she whispered, the raspiness in her voice telling of her injuries.

He turned to the sound as she set the ice pack aside and came to him. "Abel. The only thing that hurts me is not knowing what's hurting you."

He drew her carefully against him, aware as never before

of her fragility...and of an inner strength he suspected even she didn't know she possessed.

"Talk to me." She pressed her face into his shoulder. "Trust in me."

Trust. She was asking for the one thing he guarded above all else. In the face of what he'd put her through tonight, trust was the very least of what he owed her. It was what she wanted. It was what she needed. And if he gave it up, it was the one thing that could send her away.

He lifted her in his arms. Cradled her against his chest. Pressing his lips to her hair, he sat down on the sofa, holding her on his lap because he couldn't bear to let her go.

The firelight danced into the darkness. His heartbeat pounded into the silence, as he held her not knowing where to start—yet knowing where it would end.

Her small hand on his jaw brought his head down.

"I know you don't want to hear this. I know it may be too soon for you. But I can't hold it in any longer. I love you, Abel Greene."

He pinched his eyes shut against the suddenness and the sharpness of the sting.

"I love you," she repeated, the throaty rasp in her voice a reminder of the pain he'd caused. "You have to trust me enough to believe that. What you've done, where you've been, what you've endured—it's all a part of you. But it's all a part of your past. The future is what's important now. The future and what we can make it.

"But—" she swallowed past the soreness "—but if it's your past that's standing in the way of that future, then I need you to share it with me. I need to understand what I'm up against."

He covered her hand with his and pressed it against his lips. Like the feel of her skin, she was soft and pure and clean—everything he wasn't and never had been.

"And what if you can't handle what I tell you? What if you find it's so ugly and repulsive you—"

She silenced him with the press of her fingers to his lips. "What if you just trust me?"

The openness of her entreaty touched him in places he'd never allowed anyone close to. And the truth of her words allowed her access to his secrets. Secrets he'd locked inside for so long that when they broke free in his nightmares, the one person who least deserved it had gotten hurt.

He couldn't let it happen again. One way or another, he had to protect her. And he knew that by revealing his past to her, he would. With confession, came absolution. If he let the demons out of the dark, they were less likely to bother him again. The question was, would Mackenzie follow them out the door?

He didn't want to lose her. But he couldn't live with himself if he hurt her again.

"When I left here," he began, "it was with no prospects, no idea of what I was going to do with my life. And with an ultimatum to get the hell out of Dodge." He brought his hand to his jaw, ran his fingers along the scar in a knee-jerk reaction the memory that night always prompted.

"Grunewald," she whispered, her insight no longer surprising him. "He did that to you."

"Yeah. And then he made damn sure I wasn't around to tell the tale." He ran a hand along her back. She snuggled closer as he told her about how Grunewald and his pack had cornered him, leaving out the details of how bad the beating they'd given him was. Reluctantly he told her about his involvement with the woman who was now Grunewald's wife and her attempt to pick up where they'd left off when he'd come back to the lake.

"Even back then, he had the power. He wanted me gone and made it clear that if I didn't disappear, he'd convince Trisha to file rape charges against me. With the reputation

I'd so carefully cultivated, there was no doubt in my mind that they'd make them stick.''

''It's so unfair.''

''It's life,'' he stated flatly. ''And it was my wake-up call. I'd always known money talked. I decided then and there that I wanted to have a voice. To make money, I needed skills. So I joined the Marines and surprised myself and the brass by being a good one. It was the first time in my life I'd felt like I was being judged for what I could do, instead of what I was or wasn't or where I'd come from.''

He felt her smile form against his chest, close to where her small hand rested.

''What...?'' he asked.

''I'm trying to picture you without your hair.''

He covered her hand with his and held it here, savored the warmth of it seeping through his skin. ''The hair came later.''

He worked his jaw, remembering the catalyst that had spurred his decision to let it grow. ''I opted out of the Marines after my four years and joined the D.C. Police Force. Yeah,'' he said when she pulled away and with furrowed brows, looked up at him. ''Me. A cop. Only I'd had enough of uniforms and regiments by then. When the opportunity came to go undercover, I took it.''

And that's when his downward spiral had begun.

''Dangerous,'' she murmured and raised her hand to his neck and hung on tight.

He closed his eyes. Let out a deep breath. ''Yeah. Dangerous. In more ways than you can imagine. I became addicted to it. Not the drugs—the danger. The deeper the cover, the better I liked it, the more reckless I got. Before long it wasn't enough. I wanted more action—more than even the D.C. Police Force could offer. So I joined the company.''

"The company?"

"CIA."

He felt her body tense.

"It's everything you've ever heard about it, comprising both the best and the worst elements imaginable. The ideal is that everyone plays by the rules. The reality is that no matter how diligently they try to police it, there will always be a segment of the agency that is morally corrupt—loose cannons who make their own rules and draw their own lines when the bureaucratic process impedes results. It doesn't take long before some of the good guys become little better than the bad guys. And I became one of the best."

He clenched his jaw, remembering. "The day I crossed over was the day I lost my partner because the powers-that-be had been too mired in their by-the-book game plan to act. When they finally decided to move, it was too late and Carson was dead.

"I killed." The two words crashed into the tension like breaking glass. Abrupt. Brutal. Chilling. Her silence scared the hell out of him—just like his confession frightened her. He'd shocked her. But he wouldn't let himself stop. He owed her the truth. If he gave her nothing else, he'd give her that.

"I killed and I called it self-defense. I used and called it justice. I witnessed brutality I could have stopped and told myself it was for the common good. When Carson died, I accepted that I was dispensable to a government that honored me to my face for my fight against the drug war, then sent me to the wolves without conscience or care.

"A year later I got out—and went into business on my own. If I was going to put my neck on the line, I decided it might just as well be for my own gain.

"The American government wasn't the only one with an interest in curtailing the drug traffic. Many lesser powers were in need of my services, although their motives may not have been as humanitarian.

"I didn't care about their motives. I only cared about mine. Money. I contracted with anyone who was willing to meet my price—and I delivered on every dollar they paid me, earned each one twice over."

He drew a deep, unsteady breath, reliving a hundred ugly encounters, abhorring the mercenary he'd become.

"There's a village in Colombia." On this cold winter night he could still feel the suffocating heat, smell the putrid stench, see the squalor of that hell on earth thousands of miles and five years away. "It was seething with decay and ruled by the king pin of an international drug cartel. I tracked him there. Stalked him, cornered him—then made a near-fatal mistake.

"She was twelve years old." He remembered her like it was yesterday. "Her eyes were a liquid, brimming brown that spoke of innocence and invited trust. A trust I accepted. She was my source." He closed his eyes, disgusted. "A kid…and I used her to get information. Talk about justice. It turned out she was using me. She had a family to feed. So she led me into a trap. Straight into Gutierrez's den."

He was vaguely aware of the shudder rippling through him, distantly cognizant of Mackenzie's heart thudding heavily against his own—but he was vividly mired in that part of his past.

"The only reason he didn't kill me was because he was bored. I provided a diversion. When the beatings lost entertainment value for him, he experimented with electricity."

Sweat broke out on his forehead and oozed like blood down his face, into his eyes. "Then the drugs became his favorite game, his greatest source of amusement. And my living hell."

He shook himself back to the present, made himself fo-

cus on the fire and its pure, steady flame. He wrapped Mackenzie tighter in his arms, holding on to her like she was
his link to the here and now.

"Every day he promised me he'd kill me. After a month
of promises, I begged him to do it."

"How did you get away from him?" Her voice was
small and fearful.

A grim smile twisted one corner of his mouth. "I didn't.
He got away from me. The ruling political faction of the
province was taking a lot of heat from the Drug Enforce-
ment Agency. Their token gesture was to storm Gutierrez's
stronghold and run him out of the country. I was the prize
they found in his wine cellar. They turned me over to the
American Consulate figuring they'd score major points."
He laughed, a harsh, cynical sound that held a trace of the
madness he'd felt when they'd dragged him out of that dark
hole.

"The suits at the consulate were not happy to see me.
They'd known I was down there somewhere, but didn't
want to know what I was doing. I was a renegade. An
embarrassment—but I'd been one of them once, so they
hustled me quietly back to the states and tucked me neatly
away in a VA hospital in Virgina. I stayed until I was
strong enough to walk out on my own steam. Then after
holing up for a month in a seedy little motel on the outskirts
of D.C., I came back here."

The breath he let out felt symbolic of letting go of that
part of his life.

"I bought a small camper, I parked it on the land. My
body healed physically. I endured the withdrawal, I lived
through the nightmares. Gradually I got my strength back.
As therapy, more than anything, I started building the
cabin. It took me two and a half years. It took another two
before I quit sleeping with a loaded glock under my pillow
and a steel bar wedged across each door."

"And you still have the nightmares," she said, the scratchiness of her half whisper a stark testimony to that fact.

"I still have the nightmares."

She pulled away from him. Touched a hand to his face and met his eyes. He didn't see revulsion. He didn't see hatred. He saw only that she was hurting. Hurting for him. A tear slipped out, trickled down her cheek, as she pressed her face to his and whispered, "You don't have to deal with them alone anymore."

He hadn't realized he'd been holding his breath. He hadn't realized his heart had stopped beating and his mind was set to lock back into that place where the pain couldn't reach him. He hadn't realized he could still feel such stark, consuming fear.

Her softly spoken words both destroyed and resurrected him with their purity and power. His own eyes burned. His throat ached as he held her, rocked her and thanked the Fates for their generosity in sending her to him.

"Did you like the person you were back then?"

He hadn't expected the question. It showed in his response. "Did I give you any indication that I did?"

She pulled back, her smile gentle. "No. None. I just wanted to make sure you realized it. You didn't like him. You didn't approve of what he did. Neither do I." She framed his face in her hands. "But I understand him...I understand what drove him to do the things he did. And I forgive him.

"You—the man you've become—need to forgive him, too. You need to forgive the man you once were. He was a victim, Abel. And until you realize that, you'll continue to be a victim, too."

She kissed him then. A forgiving kiss. A healing kiss.

Humbled, he covered her hands with his own. "I've done

nothing to deserve you,'' he whispered, and had never felt anything so deeply in his life.

"What you deserve has nothing to do with me. What you deserve is a chance to see that you've made yourself into the kind of man circumstances were determined to keep you from becoming.''

He brought her hands to his mouth, pressed a deep kiss to her open palms. "And what you deserve is a damn sight better than me. How did you get this way? So totally accepting? So uncategorically selfless?''

Mackenzie gazed into the eyes of the man she loved. She understood the haunted looks now. She understood his pain. And she lived with a corresponding guilt.

"Not selfless,'' she amended. "Selfish.''

His dark brows furrowed in denial.

"Yes,'' she insisted, then confessed to a secret of her own. "Mark, and the danger he was in, wasn't my only motive for coming here. And I'm not as strong as you give me credit for being.''

She rose and walked to the fire. Crossing her arms under her breasts, she stared into the crackling flames, aware of his puzzled gaze tracking her.

"I was tired,'' she said in a weary voice. "Tired of being there for Mark. Of being the *only* one there for him. I wanted a life. I wanted to come and go as I pleased. I wanted to do all those things a woman my age was supposed to do but couldn't because I was—in the most literal sense of the word—my brother's keeper.''

She blinked back tears of shame. "I resented Mark because my life wasn't what I'd been promised by the purveyors of the American Dream. It took every dime I made to keep a roof over our heads—such as it was. I gave up my dream of completing my education so I could make something of myself. So I could *be* somebody.''

She shook her head, self-disgust weighing down like

lead. "The day I ran across your ad was the day I threw in the towel. I wasn't just thinking about Mark when I answered it. I was thinking about me, too. I saw a chance for someone else to share the load. I saw a chance to be taken care of instead of always being the caretaker."

She turned to him them, tears brimming. "Selfless? No. I came here because I wanted to dump the entire tired mess of my life on someone else. It was calculated. And it was self-serving. And it makes me ashamed."

He rose and went to her. "What it makes you," he said, touching a hand to her hair, "is human. With human weakness and human need. And what it makes me is damn lucky that I was the dump site."

His gentle smile was coaxing. "You love your brother, Mackenzie. No one—especially you—should ever doubt that. You saved his life when you brought him here." He curled a knuckle under her chin. "And don't ever doubt you saved mine, too."

Ten

The next morning Abel rode his snowmobile over to Crimson Falls and brought Mark home. It was time, Abel said to him, to become a family.

Mark was a little edgy at first. Mackenzie suspected it was because he was trying to get a feel for his new role in Mackenzie's life. He seemed to relax later in the day as he sensed that his status hadn't changed. She relaxed, too. He was still her little brother, and despite her feelings of guilt over her motives, she loved him and knew she would fight for his life again if it ever came to that.

As for Mackenzie, she felt safe and cared for and totally in love. She was completely enamored with her husband and the winter wonderland that was Legend Lake.

Two days after Mark's return, it was Christmas Eve. The following day they would join Scarlett and Casey at the hotel for dinner, and later in the week they'd all get together with Maggie and J.D., who were returning to the lake after spending the holiday with J.D.'s family in the Cities.

But tonight, Christmas Eve, was theirs.

The three of them had made a pact. Since both Mark and Mackenzie were flat broke, Abel wasn't allowed to spend any money on them. The gifts they ended up exchanging turned out to be far more special than anything money could have bought.

And the memories they made as they sat on the floor around the tree to open their presents were ones Mackenzie knew she'd treasure forever. She memorized every scent, every sound, every soft caress of her husband's eyes. Every nuance of excitement and anticipation Mark worked so hard to hide and had such little success in accomplishing.

This was her family. And these were the memories she wanted to cherish.

Dozens of tiny lights glittered on the branches of the Christmas tree. Outside, the window ledges were heavy with two or three inches of fresh snowfall. She'd lit candles on the hearth, had even scared up a radio station on Mark's boom box that, much to Mark's pretended dismay, played nonstop Christmas music.

Abel had moved Nashata and the pups to the rug by the hearth for the evening. Soft, snuffling grunts could be heard coming from the whelping box as the puppies wiggled their way around each other then knotted into a pile of full tummies and velvet-soft fur.

"You first, Abel," Mark said, extending an envelope.

On his own, Mark had come up with the idea of giving IOUs. For Abel there were IOUs for horse chores and help at the logging site. He gave Mackenzie a promise that he'd keep the rap music down to her definition of a tolerable level and give school his best shot when it resumed after the holidays.

Mackenzie—feeling like Betty Crocker and loving it—

had made Mark his own batch of fudge and stuffed some tins she'd found in the back of Abel's cupboards full of Christmas cookies.

"Just like 'Little House on the Prairie,'" Mark said, trying for a sputter but working harder to hide a grin as he bit into a sugar cookie bell.

For Abel, Mackenzie laid an offer on the table to straighten up his office and catch up on the book work he avoided at all costs. Her other gifts to him were of a more intimate nature which she planned to deliver in the privacy of their bedroom.

Abel's gifts, however, were the most special of them all.

To Mark, he gave one of Nashata's puppies. Tears glittered in her little brother's eyes as he croaked out a rusty thank you around the lump in his throat.

"You'll have to work it out with Casey," Abel added, as much to fill the silence and give Mark time to deal with his emotions. "I promised her the pick of the litter when we first found out about the pups. And I hear she's working Scarlett over pretty good trying to convince her to let her have two."

"Maggie's working on J.D., too," Mackenzie added. "And since he doesn't seem capable of denying her anything, I'm sure she'll get her way."

"I don't care which one—" Mark began, then stopped midsentence when Abel tugged a red ribbon from the tree and handed it to him. A key dangled from the ribbon's trailing ends.

Mark's face went white as his gaze darted from Abel's to the key.

"She's an older model," Abel said casually. "I bought her the first winter I was up here—but I think she'll run with a little work. The engine needs a tune-up and we may have to put new belts on the skis but she's yours if you want her."

"A snowmobile?" Mark whispered, sounding as if he was afraid that if he said it too loud it wouldn't be true.

Abel nodded.

When it became apparent that Mark was so overwhelmed he was either going to explode or blow his macho image to smithereens by crying, Abel came to the rescue. "She's under a tarp in the stable. Why don't you grab a flashlight and go check her out."

With soft smiles, they watched him head for the door.

Mackenzie was the one who ended up crying. Hot, salty tears leaked down her cheeks as she gazed at her husband.

"You are a very special man."

He shrugged. "It was just sitting there."

"It was just yours," she said and went to him where he sat cross-legged beside the tree. She straddled his lap, locked her legs around his waist, and looped her arms around his neck. "And you gave it to him. No one has ever done anything—"

He shushed her with a kiss. "You're not going to cry when I give you your present are you?"

She sniffed and knuckled the tears from her eyes. "Probably."

He gave her a hard hug then reached under the tree.

"Open it," he said, wedging a carefully wrapped package between them.

Slowly she worked her fingers under the tape.

"It's just paper," he said, impatient with the meticulous care she took to avoid tearing it.

"But it's paper that you used to wrap the first Christmas gift you've ever given me. I want to save it."

"And who will save me from sentimental women?"

She gave him a half-hearted cuff with her elbow and took her own sweet time.

Beneath the gold foil paper was a book. It was old and leather bound, the edges curled with time and softened by the many hands that had held it. She ran her finger tips across the aged, scarred leather.

"It was my great-great-grandmother's. Don't. Don't do that," he pleaded as the tears began again.

"I can't help it." She pinched her eyes tight, gave her head a sharp shake and tried to blink them back.

She opened the book and through a blur of tears, focused on a handwritten page. "It's...French?"

He nodded. "She was the daughter of a war chief. A Frenchman from Quebec fell in love with her and her people. He loved the stories they told, recorded them in this bound volume and gave it to her as a wedding gift."

The sweetest ache filled her chest as she held the book to her breast. "I wish I could read them."

"I'll read them to you. And we'll discover the legends together."

The tree lights reflected in his eyes as he watched her.

"Do you think Manabozho is in here?"

"I know he is," he whispered, then gave her the most precious gift of all. "Just as I know that I love you."

It was a record night for tears. And for revelations.

"I have one last thing for you," she said, getting herself together. She reached around him and produced an envelope from under the tree skirt.

He looked at it and frowned. A slow smile crept across his face when he recognized his own handwriting and it dawned on him that the letter inside was the one he'd written calling the arrangement off.

"I thought you didn't receive this."

"Guess I was mistaken," she said, watching his face carefully.

He didn't say a word. He merely rose, with her still wrapped around him, and walked to the hearth.

"Merry Christmas, wife," he murmured and tossed the letter into the fire.

"Merry Christmas, husband," she whispered against his mouth, as he drew her into a kiss that told her everything she needed to know about his love.

Trouble always found paradise. It was like an unwritten law. But as the days after Christmas passed, and her relationship with Abel solidified and settled, Mackenzie was beginning to think maybe someone else's paradise was going to be invaded this time.

The changes in Mark were heartwarming. She had Abel to thank for that. While Mark insisted he was enjoying himself—and it was obvious that he was—Abel took special care to make time for him. They got the snowmobile running and spent a good part of each day scouting the snowmobile trails that wound their way around Legend Lake. He introduced Mark to ice fishing and they brought home a walleyed pike, a delicacy Mackenzie wondered how she'd lived this long without.

But most of all, what he gave to her brother was his trust. He trusted him to go out on the snowmobile alone. He trusted him with the care of his horses and to help him at the logging site.

Those might have been small matters to some. But to a boy who had never been given the opportunity to trust in himself, they were life altering.

When Scarlett pulled in the morning after New Year's Day to pick Mark up and take him to school with Casey, Mackenzie was full of hope that his last transition would go as smoothly as the past few days they'd all spent together. And it did. The first day was eventful for its lack of events.

It was on the second day that all hell broke loose.

Abel was at the logging site when she got a call from the school a little after noon asking her to come and get Mark. There'd been an incident. She didn't think past her concern for Mark. She didn't try to reach Abel on the cellular. She snagged the keys to Abel's truck and headed for Bordertown.

The town was small—less then ten thousand people. It didn't take her long to get to the high school. She bolted through the double metal entrance doors, got her bearings and headed down the hall toward the door marked Principal's Office.

She introduced herself to a pinch-faced secretary who looked her up and down then picked up the phone.

"Mackenzie Greene is here, Dr. Chipman. Right through that door," she said stiffly when she hung up the phone.

Mackenzie had decided long ago that all principals' offices came equipped with austere, vinyl side chairs, yellowed venetian blinds and a wooden chair in the corner reserved exclusively for the troublemakers.

Her heart sank when she saw Mark occupying that designated space. His shirt was torn, his lip was bloody, his knuckles swollen. And his face was a mask of cold indifference. She knew better. He was seething beneath that "nothing can get to me" glare.

"Are you all right?" she asked, going to him.

He gave a defiant sniff and looked away.

"Your brother was involved in a bit of a scuffle after lunch today."

This from Dr. Chipman, whom she'd met and liked when she'd enrolled Mark in school over the holidays. A small man, he sat quietly behind his scarred walnut desk, his eyes magnified behind a pair of thick glasses, his receding hairline combed back unapologetically.

"The last I knew," Mackenzie said, working hard at keeping calm, "a scuffle generally requires more than one participant. Why is it, then, that Mark is the only one waiting in your office?"

Dr. Chipman smiled kindly. "It's a little rule of mine.

Divide and conquer. The other boy is waiting for his parents in the superintendent's office.''

Immediately she felt sheepish. "I'm sorry. I shouldn't have jumped to conclusions."

"Apology accepted. In the meantime I think it would be wise if you took Mark home with you today. A new school is always an adjustment—but this is not the way to settle in."

"What happened?" she asked, turning to Mark.

He was as silent as stone.

"That's about as much as we've gotten out of either him or the Grunewald boy," Dr. Chipman said. "Maybe he'll feel more like talking to you."

The blood drained from Mackenzie's face at the mention of Grunewald's name.

"John Grunewald's son?" she asked, praying the answer would be no. It came as no surprise when it wasn't.

"What happened?" she asked again, after she'd hustled Mark out of the building and into the pickup.

He stared sullenly out the window.

"Mark. You've got to tell me."

"I've got to tell you nothing. I hate this place. We never should have left California. There's nothing but snow and ice and hicks."

She felt heartsick. It was back. All of it. The anger. The stubborn chip that occupied a prize spot on his shoulder.

He wouldn't talk to her. He wouldn't let her in. Casey talked, though. When Scarlett picked her up after school, Casey told her the whole story. Scarlett retold Casey's account of the events over a cup of coffee at the Greenes' kitchen table, while Casey sought out Mark in his room.

"According to Casey, the trouble started early in the day but came to a head in the lunchroom. Mark and Casey were eating together—Ryan Grunewald evidently took exception.

"It sounds like he'd been taunting Mark all day—about everything from the length of his hair to the fact that he'd been set back a grade because of all the classes he'd missed in L.A."

Mackenzie studied Scarlett's tense expression. "Let's have the rest of it."

Reluctantly Scarlett told her. "Ryan made an off-color remark about you and Abel."

She heard the rest of it through a nauseous blur. Mark had offered the boy an opportunity to take it back. When Ryan told him in crude, graphic detail what Mark could do with his offer, Mark had flown across the table and torn into him. It had taken four teachers to pull them apart.

Mackenzie didn't have a clue how they were ever going to set things right. Abel would be so angry. She thought of his dark past, of the violence that had ruled his life, and she feared for both him and John Grunewald.

"Abel can't find out about this."

"I think it's going to be a little hard to keep it from him, don't you? According to Casey, Mark's lip is split pretty badly."

"I know. And I'll tell him about the fight. What I don't want him to know is that it was John Grunewald's son who provoked Mark. There are bad feelings between Grunewald and Abel."

Scarlett gave her a sympathetic look. "I know. Maggie told me."

"Maggie? How much does Maggie know?"

"All of it. She knows it was John who knifed Abel all those years ago. The moves John's wife put on Abel when he came back to the lake. The problems at the logging site that Abel suspects Grunewald is behind." Scarlett stopped, reacting to the stunned look Mackenzie hadn't been able to hide. "Oh. Oh, dear. You didn't know about that, did you?"

Mackenzie swallowed back a thickening lump of dread. "What problems at the logging site?" she asked, slipping deeper into a desperation too, too reminiscent of the panic that had sent her running from California.

"Tell me, Scarlett. If you're my friend, you'll tell me."

With a pained look and a reluctant sigh, Scarlett told her about the sabotage on Abel's machinery, then about the fire.

Mackenzie propped her elbows on the table and lowered her head in her hands. It was worse than she thought. Abel had said Grunewald wanted his timber. He'd even suggested Grunewald was the kind of man who would go to ugly lengths to get what he wanted. Evidently, he was also the kind of man who would pass his hatred on to his son to perpetuate. It wasn't right. And it wasn't fair. And she felt helpless to stop what was happening.

Snow had begun to fall by the time Scarlett and Casey left the cabin. Mackenzie waited for them to drive out of sight before she made up her mind to confront Grunewald herself. It was the only way to avoid more violence and keep the war between Abel and Grunewald from escalating.

Abel wouldn't like it, but she couldn't just sit back and watch while her family was pulled apart by the vindictiveness of one man.

She tried not to think about the promise she'd made Abel to stay away from Grunewald. She thought, instead, of setting things right.

Snagging the keys to the truck, she flew outside, rushing in her urgency to get to Grunewald before Abel came home and took matters into his own hands. The roar of Abel's snowmobile, followed by the sight of it cresting the rise behind the cabin, however, kept her from firing up the engine.

Swamped by a crushing weight of fear, guilt and dread,

she dropped her forehead to the back of her hands where they gripped the steering wheel.

She was still sitting that way when Abel rapped a knuckle on the driver's side window.

Slowly she raised her head. Wearily she met the concerned question in his dark eyes. Then she discarded all the cover stories she'd considered telling him.

When he opened the truck door, she took his hand. In a silence that rang with a foreshadowing of what was to come, she walked with him to the cabin.

She delivered the news with a calmness she was far from feeling, carefully watching his face as they sat opposite each other at the kitchen table. The tight set of his jaw was telling. The flinty look in his eyes warned of the danger she'd hoped to avoid.

"I should have seen this coming," he said after a long moment. "I should have known Grunewald would pass his poison on to his son."

Mackenzie felt physically ill. It was so unfair. The two people she loved most in her life were being hurt by pettiness and small-minded vindictiveness.

"You have to feel sorry for the boy," she said, reaching deep for perspective, even as she thought of Mark's battered face and the way he'd reverted to hiding behind his protective shell of indifference and anger.

"I do. But I don't have to feel sorry for his father."

Without another word Abel rose from the table and shrugged back into his jacket.

Mackenzie shot to her feet at the same time her heart dove to her stomach. "Abel, no. Please...stay away from Grunewald. Please," she insisted, clamping a hand on his arm as he reached for the door. "Don't go. We'll think of some other way to handle this."

"You were going." His eyes accused. "That's what you were doing when I found you. You were going to confront him, weren't you? If I hadn't come home when I did, that's exactly what you'd have done—even though you promised me you'd stay away from him.''

"I would never betray you, Abel." She closed her eyes. "But I wanted to help."

"I fight my own battles, Mackenzie."

"Exactly what I was trying to avoid," she countered, trying to reason with him through her plea. "A battle. There's been enough fighting. There's been enough hate. I don't want you or anyone else getting hurt because of Mark or me."

He shook his head wearily. "If you think this is about Mark or you, you're only fooling yourself."

The resolve clouding his eyes was so cold it made her shiver as he shrugged off her hand and strode out the door.

Only the snowfall, which had picked up in intensity, made the Grunewald residence difficult to find. Once Abel spotted the three sprawling stories of opulently constructed brick, towering like a monument to Grunewald's wealth at the far end of town, he pulled into the drive.

The man himself answered the door.

Abel faced his nemesis with a grim scowl. "Grunewald."

John Grunewald's eyes narrowed in surprise before his mouth twisted into an ugly facsimile of a smile.

"Well, well. Let me guess. You take a wrong turn? I guess it's understandable in this storm. You'd be wanting the other side of the tracks."

Abel clenched his jaw against the acid in Grunewald's tone, but forced himself to ignore the insult.

"We need to talk."

"Talk?" While he looked doubtful, Grunewald stepped aside, and like a king offering an audience to a serf, motioned Abel into a foyer consisting of space, a high, vaulted ceiling and a glittering cut glass chandelier.

"I'd think you'd have better—more pleasurable things to do," he added with an oily, ugly smile, "than talking with me. I heard that new wife of yours is a real sweet little piece. Congratulations must be in order—for you, anyway," he said, shutting the door behind him. "And condolences for her."

It was only the picture of Mackenzie, of the fear in her eyes as he'd left her, of her plea for no more fighting, that kept his fists doubled in his pockets instead of connecting with Grunewald's teeth.

"Look, Grunewald," he began, biting back the urge, "there's bad blood between us—"

"There is no blood between us, Greene," he said, cutting him off. "And the only bad blood, as you put it, is confined to your veins."

Abel realized in that moment that coming here had been a mistake. Grunewald wouldn't be reasoned with. He made his own reason.

Disgusted by his error in judgment, he fought back with a verbal blow of his own. "I understand you can't help being a bastard, but isn't the bigot role about played out? A man of your wealth and 'breeding' has to recognize what a social blunder that is in this day and age."

Grunewald's face hardened into a semblance of controlled anger as the barb struck home. "Did you come here to trade insults, or was there another purpose to your visit?"

Yeah. There was a purpose, Abel thought, barely holding back the anger that was determined to take center stage. *I came here to rearrange your face you sorry sonofabitch.* And as he stood there, itching to do just that, Mackenzie's words edged through again and altered his course. "There's been enough fighting," she'd said.

She was right. There had been enough. No matter how much personal satisfaction he'd feel busting Grunewald in the chops, it would only exacerbate the situation. Gathering strength from Mackenzie's conviction and making it his own, he settled himself down.

"Look...I came here to appeal to you as a parent," he said, cutting to the heart of the matter. "Your son and my wife's brother got into a fight today at school."

"So I heard," Grunewald said with an ingratiating smirk.

"It didn't have to happen. And there is no reason for it to happen again."

"Boys will be boys," Grunewald said with a shrug.

"This has nothing to do with those boys. It has to do with us, and you know it. Your quarrel is with me. What happened between us happened a long time ago. You want to keep it alive, fine. I can handle it. What I can't handle is that you've extended your anger to children."

Grunewald snorted. "That stringy-haired outlaw is hardly a child."

Abel bit down hard on his temper. "They're both children. Your son. Mackenzie's brother," he said, refusing to give Grunewald the pleasure of riling him. "And it's up to us to give them a chance to stay that way.

"They'll both grow up soon enough," he continued, when Grunewald only narrowed his eyes. "And then they'll have the opportunity to decide how to deal with attitudes like yours. I don't expect you to do anything for Mark, but I'd ask you to look deep and do something for your own son. He deserves better than the antagonism you're breeding in him."

His eyes burning with outrage, Grunewald stormed to the door and opened it wide. "I don't have to listen to this from you. And I sure as hell don't have to listen to it in my own home. Get the hell out of here."

Abel held his ground. "If you care about your son," he

said, when Grunewald's stone face showed no change of emotion, "You'll think about what I said. He deserves better."

A movement in the hallway caught Abel's eye just then. A young man, his features clearly declaring that he was John Grunewald's son, stepped out of the shadows. The pensive look on the boy's face told Abel he'd heard every word.

Grunewald glanced in the direction Abel's gaze had taken and spotted his son standing there.

"Think about what I said, Grunewald." Abel walked slowly toward the door. "And remember that what we give our children reflects both the best and the worst of us. You have a chance to give him the best of you. Don't blow it."

"Get out," Grunewald repeated forcefully.

Abel shook his head. "I'm going. You and your conscience have a real nice evening together."

Mackenzie was pacing the floor like a caged tiger by the time Abel's headlights sliced through the thick drift of falling snow and building wind.

When he shouldered inside the kitchen, shaking snow from his jacket and hair, she stood like a shadow near the sink, afraid to look—afraid to ask.

Without a word Abel crossed the room and took her into his arms.

"You can relax, little bird." He lowered his mouth to her hair. "I was a good boy."

The knots in her shoulders and neck eased with her exhaled breath. "I love you," she whispered against his shoulder.

He ran a hand up and down the length of her back. "I wanted to hit him. I wanted to pound the ever-loving life out of him for who he is and what he is—and what he's making his son."

"But you didn't."

"No." He let out a deep breath of his own. "And I didn't make a dent in his attitude, either. I'm afraid this might be just the beginning of Mark's trouble."

"We'll figure out a way to deal with it," she said. "Somehow we'll figure out a way."

The phone rang as she drew away to look in his eyes. He touched a finger to her jaw, gave her a weary smile, then reached for the phone.

"Greene," he said, snagging the receiver from its cradle.

Mackenzie watched as he listened quietly, his face tightening into a frown as he dragged a hand through his hair. "Yeah. I'll be right there."

"What?" she asked, a sense of foreboding shivering down her spine.

"That was J.D. They're organizing a search party."

She cast a look outside. The snow was falling harder and heavier. The wind added a vicious chill and compounded the diminishing visibility.

"Someone's lost in this?"

He nodded.

"How awful."

"The Grunewald boy is missing."

Her hand came involuntarily to her throat. "The Grunewald boy?"

Mark, his lip swollen and bruised, stepped out from the shadowed hallway and into the kitchen. "I want to help look for him."

Abel looked from Mackenzie's stricken face to Mark's.

"He called. Ryan," Mark clarified, responding to Mackenzie's look of disbelief. "He said he heard everything Abel told his father. He said he got to thinking that Abel was right. And he was wrong. He said he was sorry about the things he said to me about you."

Mark cast his eyes downward, his expression troubled.

"He also said he told his old man that he was going to call and apologize. The creep told him that if he did, he wasn't his son any longer."

Mackenzie covered her mouth with her hand, wrapping her other arm tightly around her waist.

"I want to help look for him," Mark repeated, and met her eyes with as much determination as appeal.

She wanted to order him to his room where he'd be safe. The storm was no place for him. He could get lost himself, and on a night like this the results could be fatal.

But as she looked at the determined set of his young face, she knew she'd lose him, anyway, if she didn't let him go.

"Don't skimp on the sweaters," Abel said at her nod. "I'll gas up the machines while you get ready."

Mark took off for his room at a run.

Abel cupped her face in his hands. "I won't let anything happen to him."

She nodded, but couldn't speak. Five minutes later they were gone.

The only thing predictable about fate is its unpredictability. It can be as fickle as it can be cruel. As twisted as it can be kind. The proof of that came when, out of the dozens of rescue teams looking for Ryan Grunewald, it was Abel and Mark who found him at midnight.

He'd wrapped his snowmobile around a tree halfway between Bordertown and a wilderness area known as Woodenfrog Landing. His blood alcohol level accounted for the empty flask they found beside the wreckage, and possibly for the fact that he'd escaped with nothing more than a broken arm and a little frostbite.

Mark and Abel wrapped him in a survival blanket and heat packs, then radioed for an ambulance that came within a half hour and transported Ryan to the Bordertown Community Hospital.

When the two of them walked through the cabin's kitchen door an hour later, they were both attacked by a wildly weeping woman who alternately railed at them for the worry they'd put her through and hugged them within an inch of their lives.

Finally satisfied that, aside from being blue with cold, they were all right, Mackenzie asked about the Grunewald boy.

"He'll be okay," Abel said, warming his hands on the mug of hot chocolate she gave him. "He's lucky the frostbite is confined to one patch on his cheek. He'll have a scar, and his arm will be in a cast for several weeks, but he'll live to tell the tale."

"Thanks to you two," she said, overcome with feelings of relief, pride and love for them both.

"What...?" she asked, when Mark and Abel shared poorly suppressed conspiratorial looks. "What aren't you telling me?"

Mark was the one who caved, a grin splitting his face as he put the cap on the story.

"Ryan's old man had offered a reward to anyone who found him. A fifty-thousand-dollar reward."

Mackenzie's eyes widened. "Fifty thousand dollars?"

"Guilt money," Abel put in. "He'd put it together that he'd been responsible for driving the boy out into this storm."

The significance of what Mark and Abel had just told her was mind-boggling. "Oh, my. What a hard pill that must have been for him to swallow...that the two of you—of all people—were the ones to find his son and claim the reward."

Abel looked thoughtful. "The truth is, I think Grunewald was so glad to see Ryan alive, he wouldn't have cared if the devil himself had brought him in. I actually found myself feeling sorry for him.''

Mackenzie's heart softened a little more at this extension of her husband's compassion.

"Abel wouldn't take the money.''

Mackenzie looked from Mark to Abel.

"I don't need his money. I didn't do it for the money. I did it for the same reason Mark did. It was the right thing to do.''

Mackenzie couldn't have loved either of them more. At least, she thought she couldn't, until the next day when John Grunewald drove through the snow drifts and paid them a visit.

When her husband accepted a humbled John Grunewald's thanks for saving his son's life, along with his long-overdue apologies for the wrongs he'd done Abel, past and present, she realized she was just beginning to learn the measure of love she felt for this man.

Eleven

The Legend Lake grapevine was responsible for yet another potluck involving the Greenes—only this time it took place at the Crimson Falls Hotel.

When Mackenzie had relayed to Scarlett the unexpected turn of events surrounding Grunewald's change of heart, Scarlett had promptly called J.D. and Maggie who had instantly declared it a wonderful reason to have a party.

Mackenzie had been enchanted by the old hotel that had been built at the turn of the century to accommodate loggers and fur traders from both Canada and the United States. She hated to leave when the time came.

As she climbed on the back of Abel's snowmobile and they followed J.D. and Maggie, with Mark leading the pack home, she waved reluctant goodbyes to Scarlett and Casey where they stood bundled in their sweaters on the wraparound veranda.

"It's such a special place," Mackenzie said later, when

both Nashata and her pups and Mark were settled in for the night and she and Abel were in bed.

She snuggled close to him. If the incentive of being held by her husband wasn't enough, the wonderful wealth of heat his big body generated was too much to resist.

"I see why you worry about Casey and Scarlett, though," she said as he drew her leg across his thigh and held it there with his hand. "It's such a big, rambling old place. And it's so isolated."

"Scarlett's tough. And as she so often reminds me, she can take care of herself."

"I know. It's just that…" She sighed, troubled.

"It's just that you'd like to see her happily married like Maggie and you?" he suggested, grinning down at her.

"Yeah. Something like that," she agreed, then put her own twist on his summation. "I'd like to see her happily married like J.D. and you."

She pushed herself up on an elbow and sought his eyes. The darkness was diluted only by the mellow, cocooning glow of a waning moon that peeked in through the bedroom window. "You are happily married…aren't you?" she added hesitantly.

He cupped her jaw and drew her mouth to his for a gentle kiss. "Am I happily married?" he whispered, watching the play of his fingers as he brushed them across her lips. "Let me see if I can tell you how happily married I am."

Tunneling his hand under the covers, he drew her tight against his side with a possessive caress. On his back, in the dark, with her cuddled as tightly as a satin sheet to a mattress, he idly stroked the smooth expanse of her bare hip.

"One of the stories my mother used to tell me was the legend of the summer birds."

She sighed into the curve of his neck, feeling loved and

lucky and enfolded in a sense of fulfillment she'd never in her life thought within her reach. "Tell me."

"Once, long ago, a wendigo—a crazed, unlucky hunter—stole the summer birds from the land. The people and the animals suffered for his cruel theft. Life became one long, bitterly cold winter. Even in the summer, snow and ice covered the land, and the people shivered in their lodges, huddled around the fires and yearned for the birds to come back and bring the warmth of the sun with them.

"But they didn't come back, because the wendigo kept them imprisoned in cages and wouldn't set them free. Finally the people and the animals held a council to decide what to do. It was the fisher—one of the smallest of the animals—who volunteered to go in search of the wendigo and free the summer birds."

The story was so lovely, his voice so soft as he stroked her back and let the tale unfold.

"He went on a long journey, suffered much hardship but finally found the wendigo's lodge. In the dark of night he snuck into the wigwam while the wendigo slept. Very quietly he opened the cages and set the summer birds free. As each one flew away from its prison, the air warmed a little, the snow began to melt, the plants broke through and flowers blossomed. The summer birds, happy in their freedom, flew farther and farther north, bringing summer with them and melting the ice and the bitterness the people had felt in their hearts."

He leaned over her, his black hair spilling across his shoulder and trailing over her breasts. "To ask if I'm a happily married man is to ask if the people were happy to have the summer return to their lives.

"Yes, wife, I'm happy. You are my summer bird. You flew into my life with your warmth and your spirit, and you melted the ice that had hardened in my soul."

Tears misted her eyes as she looked into the face of this

man who had introduced her to a love as boundless and magical as the legends of the Chippewa. "And you are my Manabozho." She wound a fistful of his hair around her hand and drew his mouth to hers. "My miracle worker who can warm my heart on the coldest winter night."

"Never fly away from me, little bird," he whispered against her lips.

"This is my home," she said, responding to the depth of his need and the truth of his heart. "And you are my life. I've waited so long for both. Now that I've found you, there's no place on earth I would ever want to go."

His dark eyes glittered in the moonlit room.

"Make love to me," she said, pulling his body over hers. "Let me give you something I couldn't live without any more than I could live without you. Let me give you my heart."

He took it humbly, with gentleness and need, with passion and fire. But above all else, he took it with trust and with a love that would bind him to his summer bird forever.

*   *   *   *   *

Look for THE BRIDE OF CRIMSON FALLS,
the third book in Cindy Gerard's sensuous series,
NORTHERN LIGHTS BRIDES, *June 1997.*
Only from Silhouette Desire.

Silhouette's newest series

YOURS TRULY

Love when you least expect it.

Where the written word plays a vital role in uniting couples—you're guaranteed a fun and exciting read every time!

Look for Marie Ferrarella's upcoming Yours Truly, *Traci on the Spot*, in March 1997.

Here's a special sneak preview....

1

Morgan Brigham slowly set down his coffee cup on the kitchen table and stared at the comic strip in the center of his paper. It was nestled in among approximately twenty others that were spread out across two pages. But this was the only one he made a point of reading faithfully each morning at breakfast.

This was the only one that mirrored *her* life.

He read each panel twice, as if he couldn't trust his own eyes. But he could. It was there, in black and white.

Morgan folded the paper slowly, thoughtfully, his mind not on his task. So Traci was getting engaged.

The realization gnawed at the lining of his stomach. He hadn't a clue as to why.

He had even less of a clue why he did what he did next.

Abandoning his coffee, now cool, and the newspaper, and ignoring the fact that this was going to make him late for the office, Morgan went to get a sheet of stationery from the den.

He didn't have much time.

Traci Richardson stared at the last frame she had just drawn. Debating, she glanced at the creature sprawled out on the kitchen floor.

"What do you think, Jeremiah? Too blunt?"

The dog, part bloodhound, part mutt, idly looked up from his rawhide bone at the sound of his name. Jeremiah gave her a look she felt free to interpret as ambivalent.

"Fine help you are. What if Daniel actually reads this and puts two and two together?"

Not that there was all that much chance that the man who had proposed to her, the very prosperous and busy Dr. Daniel Thane, would actually see the comic strip she drew for a living. Not unless the strip was taped to a bicuspid he was examining. Lately Daniel had gotten so busy he'd stopped reading anything but the morning headlines of the *Times*.

Still, you never knew. "I don't want to hurt his feelings," Traci continued, using Jeremiah as a sounding board. "It's just that Traci is overwhelmed by Donald's proposal and, see, she thinks the ring is going to swallow her up." To prove her point, Traci held up the drawing for the dog to view.

This time, he didn't even bother to lift his head.

Traci stared moodily at the small velvet box on the kitchen counter. It had sat there since Daniel had asked her to marry him last Sunday. Even if Daniel never read her comic strip, he was going to suspect something eventually. The very fact that she hadn't grabbed the ring from his hand and slid it onto her finger should have told him that she had doubts about their union.

Traci sighed. Daniel was a catch by any definition. So what was her problem? She kept waiting to be struck by that sunny ray of happiness. Daniel said he wanted to take care of her, to fulfill her every wish. And he was even willing to let her think about it before she gave him her answer.

Guilt nibbled at her. She should be dancing up and down, not wavering like a weather vane in a gale.

Pronouncing the strip completed, she scribbled her signature in the corner of the last frame and then sighed. Another week's work put to bed. She glanced at the pile of mail on the counter. She'd been bringing it in steadily from the mailbox since Monday, but the stack had gotten no farther than her kitchen. Sorting letters seemed the least heinous of all the annoying chores that faced her.

Traci paused as she noted a long envelope. Morgan Brigham. Why would Morgan be writing to her?

Curious, she tore open the envelope and quickly scanned the short note inside.

Dear Traci,

I'm putting the summerhouse up for sale. Thought you might want to come up and see it one more time before it goes up on the block. Or make a bid for it yourself. If memory serves, you once said you wanted to buy it. Either way, let me know. My number's on the card.

Take care,
Morgan

P.S. Got a kick out of *Traci on the Spot* this week.

Traci folded the letter. He read her strip. She hadn't known that. A feeling of pride silently coaxed a smile to her lips. After a beat, though, the rest of his note seeped into her consciousness. He was selling the house.

The summerhouse. A faded white building with brick trim. Suddenly, memories flooded her mind. Long, lazy afternoons that felt as if they would never end.

Morgan.

She looked at the far wall in the family room. There was a large framed photograph of her and Morgan standing before the summerhouse. Traci and Morgan. Morgan and

Traci. Back then, it seemed their lives had been permanently intertwined. A bittersweet feeling of loss passed over her.

Traci quickly pulled the telephone over to her on the counter and tapped out the number on the keypad.

* * * * *

Look for TRACI ON THE SPOT
by Marie Ferrarella, coming to
Silhouette YOURS TRULY
in March 1997.

MILLION DOLLAR SWEEPSTAKES
OFFICIAL RULES
NO PURCHASE NECESSARY TO ENTER

1. To enter, follow the directions published. Method of entry may vary. For eligibility, entries must be received no later than March 31, 1998. No liability is assumed for printing errors, lost, late, non-delivered or misdirected entries.

   To determine winners, the sweepstakes numbers assigned to submitted entries will be compared against a list of randomly, preselected prize winning numbers. In the event all prizes are not claimed via the return of prize winning numbers, random drawings will be held from among all other entries received to award unclaimed prizes.

2. Prize winners will be determined no later than June 30, 1998. Selection of winning numbers and random drawings are under the supervision of D. L. Blair, Inc., an independent judging organization whose decisions are final. Limit: one prize to a family or organization. No substitution will be made for any prize, except as offered. Taxes and duties on all prizes are the sole responsibility of winners. Winners will be notified by mail. Odds of winning are determined by the number of eligible entries distributed and received.

3. Sweepstakes open to residents of the U.S. (except Puerto Rico), Canada and Europe who are 18 years of age or older, except employees and immediate family members of Torstar Corp., D. L. Blair, Inc., their affiliates, subsidiaries, and all other agencies, entities, and persons connected with the use, marketing or conduct of this sweepstakes. All applicable laws and regulations apply. Sweepstakes offer void wherever prohibited by law. Any litigation within the province of Quebec respecting the conduct and awarding of a prize in this sweepstakes must be submitted to the Régie des alcools, des courses et des jeux. In order to win a prize, residents of Canada will be required to correctly answer a time-limited arithmetical skill-testing question to be administered by mail.

4. Winners of major prizes (Grand through Fourth) will be obligated to sign and return an Affidavit of Eligibility and Release of Liability within 30 days of notification. In the event of non-compliance within this time period or if a prize is returned as undeliverable, D. L. Blair, Inc. may at its sole discretion, award that prize to an alternate winner. By acceptance of their prize, winners consent to use of their names, photographs or other likeness for purposes of advertising, trade and promotion on behalf of Torstar Corp., its affiliates and subsidiaries, without further compensation unless prohibited by law. Torstar Corp. and D. L. Blair, Inc., their affiliates and subsidiaries are not responsible for errors in printing of sweepstakes and prize winning numbers. In the event a duplication of a prize winning number occurs, a random drawing will be held from among all entries received with that prize winning number to award that prize.

5. This sweepstakes is presented by Torstar Corp., its subsidiaries and affiliates in conjunction with book, merchandise and/or product offerings. The number of prizes to be awarded and their value are as follows: Grand Prize — $1,000,000 (payable at $33,333.33 a year for 30 years); First Prize — $50,000; Second Prize — $10,000; Third Prize — $5,000; 3 Fourth Prizes — $1,000 each; 10 Fifth Prizes — $250 each; 1,000 Sixth Prizes — $10 each. Values of all prizes are in U.S. currency. Prizes in each level will be presented in different creative executions, including various currencies, vehicles, merchandise and travel. Any presentation of a prize level in a currency other than U.S. currency represents an approximate equivalent to the U.S. currency prize for that level, at that time. Prize winners will have the opportunity of selecting any prize offered for that level; however, the actual non U.S. currency equivalent prize if offered and selected, shall be awarded at the exchange rate existing at 3:00 P.M. New York time on March 31, 1998. A travel prize option, if offered and selected by winner, must be completed within 12 months of selection and is subject to: traveling companion(s) completing and returning of a Release of Liability prior to travel; and hotel and flight accommodations availability. For a current list of all prize options offered within prize levels, send a self-addressed, stamped envelope (WA residents need not affix postage) to: MILLION DOLLAR SWEEPSTAKES Prize Options, P.O. Box 4456, Blair, NE 68009-4456, USA.

6. For a list of prize winners (available after July 31, 1998) send a separate, stamped, self-addressed envelope to: MILLION DOLLAR SWEEPSTAKES Winners, P.O. Box 4459, Blair, NE 68009-4459, USA.

In February, Silhouette Books is proud
to present the sweeping, sensual new novel
by bestselling author

CAIT LONDON

about her unforgettable family—*The Tallchiefs.*

TALLCHIEF FOR KEEPS

Everyone in Amen Flats, Wyoming, was talking about
Elspeth Tallchief. How she wasn't a thirty-three-year-old
virgin, after all. How she'd been keeping herself warm at
night all these years with a couple of secrets. And now one
of those secrets had walked right into town, sending
everyone into a frenzy. But Elspeth knew he'd come for
the *other* secret....

"Cait London is an irresistible storyteller..."

—*Romantic Times*

Don't miss TALLCHIEF FOR KEEPS by Cait London, available
at your favorite retail outlet in February from

CLST

Harlequin and Silhouette celebrate
Black History Month with seven terrific titles,
featuring the all-new *Fever Rising*
by Maggie Ferguson
(Harlequin Intrigue #408) and
A Family Wedding by Angela Benson
(Silhouette Special Edition #1085)!

Also available are:
Looks Are Deceiving by Maggie Ferguson
Crime of Passion by Maggie Ferguson
Adam and Eva by Sandra Kitt
Unforgivable by Joyce McGill
Blood Sympathy by Reginald Hill

On sale in January at your favorite
Harlequin and Silhouette retail outlet.

Look us up on-line at: http://www.romance.net   BHM297

*If you're looking for irresistible
heroes, the search is over....*

Joan Elliott Pickart's

Tux, Bram and Blue Bishop and their pal,
Gibson McKinley, are four unforgettable men...on a
wife hunt. Discover the women who steal their
Texas-size hearts in this enchanting four-book series,
which alternates between Silhouette Desire
and Special Edition:

In February 1997, fall in love with Tux, Desire's
Man of the Month, in TEXAS MOON, #1051.

In May 1997, Blue meets his match in TEXAS DAWN,
Special Edition #1100.

In August 1997, don't miss Bram's romance in
TEXAS GLORY—coming to you from Desire.

And in December 1997, Gib takes more than marriage
vows in TEXAS BABY, Special Edition's
That's My Baby! title.
You won't be able to resist
Joan Elliott Pickart's TEXAS BABY.

BBOYS

COMING NEXT MONTH

As seen on TV!
Free Gift Offer

With a Free Gift proof-of-purchase from any Silhouette® book, you can receive a beautiful cubic zirconia pendant.

This gorgeous marquise-shaped stone is a genuine cubic zirconia—accented by an 18" gold tone necklace.

(Approximate retail value $19.95)

Send for yours today...
compliments of ▼ *Silhouette*®
™

To receive your free gift, a cubic zirconia pendant, send us one original proof-of-purchase, photocopies not accepted, from the back of any Silhouette Romance™, Silhouette Desire®, Silhouette Special Edition®, Silhouette Intimate Moments® or Silhouette Yours Truly™ title available in February, March and April at your favorite retail outlet, together with the Free Gift Certificate, plus a check or money order for $1.65 U.S./$2.15 CAN. (do not send cash) to cover postage and handling, payable to Silhouette Free Gift Offer. We will send you the specified gift. Allow 6 to 8 weeks for delivery. Offer good until April 30, 1997 or while quantities last. Offer valid in the U.S. and Canada only.

Free Gift Certificate

Name: _____

Address: _____

City: _____ State/Province: _____ Zip/Postal Code: _____

Mail this certificate, one proof-of-purchase and a check or money order for postage and handling to: SILHOUETTE FREE GIFT OFFER 1997. In the U.S.: 3010 Walden Avenue, P.O. Box 9077, Buffalo NY 14269-9077. In Canada: P.O. Box 613, Fort Erie, Ontario L2Z 5X3.

FREE GIFT OFFER
ONE PROOF-OF-PURCHASE
084-KFD

To collect your fabulous FREE GIFT, a cubic zirconia pendant, you must include this original proof-of-purchase for each gift with the properly completed Free Gift Certificate.

084-KFD

You're About to Become a *Privileged Woman*

Reap the rewards of fabulous free gifts and benefits with proofs-of-purchase from Silhouette and Harlequin books

Pages & Privileges™

It's our way of thanking you for buying our books at your favorite retail stores.

PROOF OF PURCHASE
SD-PP22
Offer expires March 31, 1997

**Harlequin and Silhouette—
the most privileged readers in the world!**

For more information about Harlequin and Silhouette's PAGES & PRIVILEGES program call the Pages & Privileges Benefits Desk: 1-503-794-2499